DOWN MEMORY LANE

PRANJALI TAYAL GUPTA

INDIA • SINGAPORE • MALAYSIA

ISBN 979-8-89673-458-1

This Book is dedicated to my father.

"A father's tears and fears are unseen, his love is unexpressed, but his care and protection remain as a pillar of strength throughout our lives."

We love you and miss you every day, papa!

Contents

CHAPTER 1

The Beginning of a Life

"And suddenly you just know it's time to start something new and trust the magic of new beginnings".

"Morning ma! Jai-Jai ram, Papa!" As Priya steps into the dining area after getting ready to leave for college on a warm April morning, pursuing her second year in Bachelor of Arts, who later on plans to learn designing or maybe teach or write. Although she is a bold, pretty, confident girl, who loves to drive. She is sometimes hot headed but loves being on adventures. Is a go-getter, strong willed girl. As she is about to take her seat, he stops to see an A4 size paper just lying there with a picture. She picks it up to read and without reading the name she looks at the picture and just swings it away, letting it fly and it drops on the floor.

"Who is this ma? Why is the man in the picture looking like a father of four!? Is papa planning to keep an accountant or a compounder?"

Priya's mom comes out of the kitchen, surprised to hear her daughter taunt and does not like the tone in her voice. But calmly as any mom would do, sits her down to explain about the whole scenario. "Beta, your grandma has been looking for a boy for you. This boy you just saw the picture of is a businessman and lives with his family. All she wants you to do is simply read his bio data, think and let us know if you want to go on to the next step. That is all. Swinging the picture away like that would do us no good, na!"

"But ma, he looks like a father of I don't know how many kids! And am I being so much of a burden to you or grandma that you want to get rid of me so quickly?! What have I done wrong that I am being asked to do all this?"

The mother cuts her daughter short, "Priya, never think that you are a burden to us. We love you a lot. We just feel you are so laid back in life, you want someone to enjoy the life with. I got married early. I am not saying you should too. Overall, this process will take time. Nobody is asking you to get married with the first boy you see. As of now, you will read about the guy, then you will get to meet him, and maybe in that meeting itself you might just decide if it's a no or a yes. And if at any point of time you feel you don't want to continue, I promise you this that no matter what, I will never persuade you to carry on. According to her, you are almost nearing the right age; it takes a lot of time in deciding too, from both sides. And above this, if you have anyone else in mind, if you like someone, I think this is the time that you should let us know, before it's too late, you know. It is all up to you. Take your own time and let us know whatever you decide."

"Ma, as of now, being really honest, I have no intentions of settling down with anyone. I just wish that I am allowed to pursue in whatever field I want after my exams. You see,

I do have some wishes and dreams, I want to live a solo life. Why would anyone want me to be dumped with an unknown person? I know myself, I know my friend Mira, Saket, who would support me. I want to see the world without a husband. I want to go on trips with you and my friends. Please understand this ma, let me live the life that you weren't able to. I love you all so much, just don't ruin this."

Upon hearing and discussion, Priya's mom pulls her hand and hugs her, and says, "I love you too sweetheart. I am so sorry; I will not bring this up again soon. You take your time and go and enjoy yourself."

And Priya plans in her head that time is what she will take. As the idea of settling down is not what she requires at present. She suddenly looks at the time and knows that it is too late for her to go to college, she calls up her friend Mira and plans to bunk that day to vent out her frustration.

"Hey Mira, where are you?"

"Stuck in traffic, I am so fudging late, God, I am so hating this right now! Why, what's up with you, you sound weird, all ok?"

"Yeah, so let's skip today, knowing we are late, I am in no mood to get scolded for this stupid thing. What say, let's go to someplace and hang out today!?" says Priya sounding super devilish.

"Umm, alright. I guess you're right about the 'not-in-the-mood-to-get-scolded' part. So, I believe I'll be there in about 20 odd minutes. I'll buzz once I reach near your place, ok?"

Priya goes back to her room, thinking that if Mira has said 20, it'll most certainly take her more time to reach her place. Staying in Delhi has its perks. Heavy traffic, people honking, Punjabis stepping out of their cars ready to pounce or put a dent!

She realises that thinking all this has made her head heavy and is beginning to ache a little on one side. But she doesn't bother much. So, Priya takes out her diary, only to jot down the prior episode.

"Dear diary,

Today's episode made me feel hurt. I get this feeling that I am a burden to my parents. I mean I might be wrong in thinking so, because they sure do love me. I remember, on my last birthday, they gifted me with the latest Nokia 6600, which I was so desperate to get. And the same year, papa gifted my brother a PS 1 and me the good old video game with all the games like 'Super Mario, Contra, Tank, Tetris...that me and Vedant (my brother) used to play when we were in school and beat each other at it....and then we outgrew it. That used to be fun! My mom helped me decorate and set up my room the first year of college as a token of appreciation for scoring well in 12th boards and getting placed in a good college; with a small television, with no satellite connection though, but a DVR cum cd player, and also knowing about my love for music, placing her own bought cassette cum cd music player with amplifier sub-woofer speakers, that to this day I haven't been able to place them nicely. And haven't really had much time to turn on the television. And I even remember, papa made sure I learnt to drive last year and I got my license. That was hilariously a great time!

Coming to what I was thinking, I sometimes feel, are all girls supposed to be married off the moment they turn the age?? Does this kind of thing happen with the boys as well? Do they go through this episode as well? I seriously wonder if the mother of a boy who has turned to the age of getting married, is being told to find a girl, forcibly or making them go through the emotional blackmail!!

I sure do know that in small villages, this is actually the condition of the parents, where the father who has, about three daughters, who have to be given away. Or is forced to give away with a good deal, as they are mostly insane or in need! Thinking all this makes me dizzy! All I want is to have a life of my own and live free of all the crap that happens in the Indian society! Maybe I will do what I think, or maybe I won't! I hope and I just pray all is fine tomorrow and things are peachy.... I know my parents are not like those.... I know they understand and care for me and Vedant."

And while she is into her own world, her phone tinkles twice, seeing the name, she quickly hides her diary and grabs her bag and walks out the door saying, "Ma, I'll be home by 8. Don't make dinner for me." And hearing her makes her mom go mad, which makes her father say, only to make his wife smile, "Let's buy a car for our daughter. She has grown up to be independent."

Mom says, "Let's not spoil her so much, it'll be quite difficult for her to leave us! You just don't understand anything." The father immediately responds, "What good would that do to her, this is her final year, we have to let her live her life. She wants to be independent. Why can't we give her that? What is the hurry? Maybe she'll find someone one day and let us know. I feel it is way too early for us to be settling her down in a marriage! I believe I will talk to my mother and let her know-it's not happening!"

Meanwhile, Mira, who is in her car, her latest model of the "beetle by Volkswagen" makes Priya get the envious vibe in her!

"Would you like to drive the car, Priya? I am way overwhelmed with all the traffic, yaah! You are my bestie, so why not!"

"Are you sure, Mira?" Asks Priya, seeming overly surprised and shocked at the same time! "I do love your car, but, it's yours and what if I bang it against someone or some car? Aren't you scared?"

"I am, way more than you think, it took some guts to even speak those words! But honestly, technically it's my dad's and he has sort of gifted it to me, and I know if anything happens to the car, I'll be grounded for life, but then what the hell! I am totally aware that you totally love this car and it's not like I am giving it away or anything, it's just I am sort of letting you drive it! What are friends for after all, right!?"

"Yeah! Okay, so you will have to just tell me where the clutch and all is! I haven't driven this thing ever, you know!" jokes Priya but Mira isn't amused.

"What....are you seriously kidding me? You really don't know where all Th....e....Pri....you...."

"I am kidding M, hahaha.... ha...ha.... got you!! Omg, that was cool!! Dude I seriously needed this today!! Hahahahaha!! I can't stop laughing!! This is super cool! Wow...I didn't know I'd beat the s#$^ out of you!"

"YOU ARE SO GONNA GET IT NA PRIYA!! I MEAN IT!! THIS WAS SO NOT COOL!! Anyway, are we going somewhere or what? You want me to crash at your place tonight?"

"Yeah, yeah, we are going! Let's go to.... wait...what?? You're crashing here tonight? Seriously?" asks stunned Priya.

"Well, yeah. Let's study for our exams together and chill out after that. We have the weekend together. Our exam isn't till May. So, we have plenty of time. Then we are the free birds for a whole month, dude! My dad's planning a trip to Dubai. That is going to be awesome! But that is much, much later. What say we have some fun today just to get our minds straight! So, where're you taking us Priya?" Mira sounds really excited.

"Well, haven't really given it a thought of where we'd be heading, all I know is I told my mom that I'll be having dinner out....so where would you suggest we head?" Priya, while saying this is taking a feel of the wheel, like caressing a baby. And suddenly she jumps, as if thinking out loud and says, "How about we go have something to eat at a cafe first, because I am starving and craving for a yummy sandwich with some coffee to go with it. What about you, M? You with me?"

"Of course, Priya, let's go and freak out. Call it your day sweetie!" and they head off to a cafe in CP, where it nearly takes them an hour to reach. Like I said before, Delhi and its traffic, a killer! She realises her headache is beginning to grow a little.

* * * * *

CHAPTER 2

The Cafe

"Sometimes, you just need a break in a beautiful place, alone to figure everything out."

It's a little over 11 am and the queue at the counter is beyond imagination! Priya is way too excited to think about the queue, and lost in her thoughts of how she would be spending the day. She then stares at people at the other side of the counter managing the different food items, which are being ordered by the people at her side of the counter. Until she hears a girl call out to her saying, "Ma'am, can I take your order...excuse me ma'am...can I take your order please?"

"Huh.... yeah.... sorry...I will have a cappuccino with a tomato sandwich-toasted please and an iced tea with the same sandwich-tomato and toasted, please, thank you."

"Anything else...?" asks the girl, as if she wants to fill me up and make me into a pig.

"No, that'll be all, thanks. How much would that be?"

"Ma'am, you can pay later. One of us will serve you, you just let us know where you're sitting." Says the girl who I think is trying to make up.

"That's awesome, what's your name.... Neha. Thank you so much." Priya thinks to herself of tipping her if she comes out to serve.

Priya then heads towards Mira, where she bumps into someone, who drops the books on to her foot, luckily Priya is in her sneakers, where she doesn't get hurt, and bends down to pick up the books to hand them over, and sees quite a good looking slender, fair, good smelling, husky voiced guy, "You okay miss, I am so sorry, I didn't see you. Are you hurt? Thanks for the books." But Priya is way over her head, and can't stop looking at the guy. Mira, who has been looking at all this from the word get-go, comes running towards them. "Hey Sameer, what are you doing here? Well, I apologise in her place, you okay Sameer? Did you get hurt? We got to go, see you later."

Mira drags Priya away, to get to their place. No sooner, they get their order, before they can even discuss about the "bang". Priya takes a large bite of her sandwich and can't stop thinking about what just happened. Just then Mira interrupts her thoughts, "Priya", where are you lost dude? You haven't said a word, what's going on in your head...you have got to talk to me. In the morning when you called, you sounded upset, then suddenly you were okay and all chirpy, after I said I would crash at your place, you were lost at the ordering counter, what is going on, and just a while ago you bumped into some random guy and haven't said a word? What...you have got to tell me honey, we have been friends for the past 1 year. And I know you. You have never been like this before. Please tell me. Is it that time of the month that you're having mood swings?"

"What....no no..." claims Priya. "I am totally okay. Nothing is wrong. I am not lost anywhere Mira. There's just too much on my mind lately. I promise you, nothing's wrong, seriously."

"I don't believe you, Priya. You just said there's too much in your mind...what is it? You know you can tell me."

"Yeah, I know, you are my pillar, Mira. I love that about you. I do remember the circumstances that made us get closer. But right now, I am just overwhelmed; there are way too many thoughts in my mind. Everything would get jumbled up if I talk, so for now all I can think about is that guy, what was his name.... Sameer...was it? And I have a feeling I have seen him somewhere. He looked familiar yet so handsome!"

"OH wow, I am asking you a serious question here, and this is what you come up with? Dude, you are...."

"M, I am just asking who that guy is, that's all. You know him, how?"

"Okay, fine, he is our neighbour; he lives across the street...from where I live. He's a sweet guy. Has 2 younger sisters and they belong to a wealthy family. My mom and his mom, and other moms have their so called "kitty parties" together. He has always been a brilliant kid from the start, drives a Royal Enfield, I am not too sure but I think he wants to join his father's business. This much I think I know."

"Wow, Mira. All I know is he sounds yummy, smells great, looks pretty handsome and most of all, drives a Royal Enfield!!!......That is just wow!!!!

And are you going out with this guy?"

"No way!! Never..." Priya cuts her in between, "Dude, never say NEVER. You know you never know where that might lead you."

"Yeah, I know Dumbo. But he is not my type. He is way too simple and down to earth. I would prefer a sturdy guy. A little like him, but definitely not him."

Priya is still not sure, "Dude, are you completely sure? I can't stop thinking about the guy. Because the way you just described him to me is, he certainly seems my type, I guess. Actually, I am not so sure what type I want. In fact, I have never even had to imagine. By the way, look what we were talking about, I am getting the goose bumps!! We are discussing a guy! Which makes me want to spill my heart out now to you, Mira...."

"In the morning, when you called...me and my mom had an argument about me getting married? An arranged marriage...can you even imagine!?!? Me... Getting married at this time.... dude what about my life...did she even bother to ask if I want to even get married or do I want that life!?! I am just sick of this mentality of people who want to just get rid of the burdens and be happy.... if they want to be happy why get married in the first place or even if they get married...why give birth even!! I just can't understand...." Tears fill her eyes. Mira comes closer to give her a hug saying, "There, there now Priya...it's ok.... they are not going to get you married so soon.... they won't.... I'll talk to them...Okay...if you want me to? Anything else you want to say...you want to get your mind lighter...some more? You can tell me, honey!"

Priya cuts her short, "Mira...let's open up a cafe...you and me...we can run it beautifully...our own small cafe...we can be our own bosses and you know we can have a nice chef...someone to take the order and run it...someone to run the accounts...it's going to be just fantastic!!! I mean... what could be wrong in this? You know what I mean!! I am pretty sure; nobody would want to stop us or talk us out of it. I think I have just realised I want to do this only...."

Mira snaps her out of her fantasy world by slapping her face gently. "Dude, chill...let's take a few easy steps...where did you get this idea from...look from what you started to talk and where you have ended...take a breath...I have no clue what has come over you...I am surprised at so many thoughts you have had in the last hour...It is unimaginable. You seem to be overwhelmed with thoughts and ideas... chill out...we are here to freak out, remember?"

"Mira, you are not listening to me. This thing is giving me the vibe.... the feeling that you know you've got to do! Maybe I had it in me...Maybe it just came...but I know for sure that this is what I plan to do...are you in it...with me or not? Look, we are going to be finishing up with our college next year, then we go on for a break for a month and a half, almost, till we start our internship, go work for companies...Blah blah...wouldn't it be better that we decide and go with the plan?! It may take us 5 years to master something that we are not even prepared for right now, but I am sure we will have help..."

Mira interrupts, "Priya, I hear you. I also understand... but don't you think we should be knowing the ABCs of opening a café?! Where will we get the investment, where can we open it....and in this crowded city... Have you even thought about it? It's going to be an endless process, honey! I am with you...but somehow you are thinking the toughest thing for us to do!!!"

"How is it tough, Mira?" Priya sounds delusional.

"Well, for starters, we need an empty plot or a property dealer or an investor...an empty space...then to set up the place...we need a decorator.... then we need the appliances.... and the list goes on....it is never ending...what if one of us loses interest in it and leave before it even starts...?!?! I am not really sure..."

"Okay Mira, let's just say it is actually going to be tough...but what if while we are at it...we might start to enjoy. I mean, who have you heard, has not enjoyed setting up a place for them?! Let's just start the process after our exams and start with the planning, partner.... what say?" exclaimed Priya.

"Alright, if you want it so bad...let's get set go then!" Agrees Mira.

And off they head to the movies, where they get disheartened as the house was full and they were too late.

So, then they head back to Priya's home to relax. As soon as they enter, they find that Priya's mom is in her private room, painting away, her brother is busy on his PS, and her father is off at the hospital with his patients. It's nearly 4 pm, Priya grabs a soda and some chips and heads to her room where Mira is lying on her bed, fast asleep. Priya also feels a bit exhausted; she crashes next to Mira and dozes off.

Mira and Priya, wake up close to midnight, hungry. Priya says yawning, "Wow, how long did we sleep off for?!" She looks at the time, and is surprisingly shocked, and calls out, "Mira, wake up. It's 11 pm!! We slept all evening and through dinner! Wake up, dude! I wonder what my parents must be thinking!"

"That you were really tired, what else must she think!! She must have come up to check and found us fast asleep, I am pretty sure she must have tried to wake us up, but we didn't so...You need to chillax, dude!! It's not like you were sleeping with a guy...huh!!" chuckles Mira.

"Shush, will you!" Says Priya.

"Dude, I guess I am hungry. Let's go check if there's anything we can eat. Then maybe we can sit and at least start studying for our last exam."

Priya agrees and they both head down to the kitchen where Priya's mom had laid the table, which had only two plates. But the food was in the fridge. So, they take out the bowls wrapped with a plastic wrap and foil, warm the food, take the chapattis and start eating without making much noise.

"Dude, your mom cooks yum food!! She might like to join our business, no!" exclaims Mira, sounding childish.

"No yaarr, she might guide us, even though I am learning from her. She does have multiple recipe books and must be having some recipes of her own as well. We could ask her tomorrow or maybe after the exam. You remember no, we had a small argument today?! I am not sure if she'll be happy about any of it." Says Priya sadly.

While they are relishing their food, Priya's father steps down to check, after hearing all the chattering and munching.

Priya gets startled and says, "Ohh papa, did we wake you up? I am so sorry. We just suddenly woke up. I am not sure how come we dozed off and...." Her father cuts her off and says, "No worries beta. I was wondering when you girls would wake up as your mom was worried you hadn't had your dinner. Are you both feeling fresh now or will you both sleep and wake up at 5 am? I have a news to share..."

"Yes papa. Yes uncle. Please do tell." They both speak simultaneously.

"Well, I was actually told to not do so, but I booked a car for Priya today! I have been doing this research about city cars, and you have been commuting in autos, bus and with Mira, so I thought why not give you a chance to drive by yourself now. We made you learn driving, and you did well, but I felt you weren't getting enough practice. It should hopefully arrive by the end of next month.... which is May."

"Aaaaaaaaaaah! Papa!!!! A car for me!!!!! You are the best, papa!!" yells Priya in excitement, literally waking up everyone.

"Sshhhhh Priya!!! I am sure now you definitely must have woken up your mother and your brother. And you are going to get in trouble now!"

"I am sorry, papa! You must have known to not share this news now. And plus, we are nowhere near my birthday nor any good news or anything, then how come...?" Priya whispers now.

"I was just feeling happy and I want you to achieve your aim. Whatever you want to do, I will support you, just remember this."

Just then her brother wakes up hearing all the noise, rubbing his eyes he enters the kitchen, looks at everyone, opens the fridge and gulps down the water directly from the bottle, despite mom telling us to not do that! But then who has obliged every time?! And then walks back to his room, waving at them.

It's nearly midnight, Mira starts yawning again, and seeing her yawn, Priya also yawns. Seeing this, Priya's father commands them both to go back to sleep. Priya asks her father when would he go to sleep, he replies he'll sleep after he finishes a report on a patient. Priya hugs her father and says, "Goodnight papa, love you."

"Goodnight sweetheart, love you, bete." Replies her father.

Mira slams on to the bed, murmuring, "Please someone turn off the lights". Priya entering the room, turns off the light and crashes on her bed next to Mira.

* * * * *

CHAPTER 3

My Friends for Life – Mira & Saket

'There are friends, there is family, and then there are friends that become family.'
'Best friends make the good times better and the hard times easier.'

It's kind of a bit difficult to explain about her, actually. She is a chirpy, funny, bold, gorgeous looking, weird, unpredictable girl! Must say, not vicious, a bit vindictive, but not with me! Have seen her go crazyyy to angry to lovable! I know it is sounding weird. Right! But then I am glad we became friends in weird circumstances. I honestly wish I should have found her earlier. Sounds too filmy, I know! But what is right, is I know it in my heart that she is my friend for life. Honestly, in my school days, I never really had friends like her. I was always on a lookout to have a friend like Mira. I used to envy most of my classmates who took each other as best mates. I even know that some of them used to pretend to be best friends, and some were calling each other close friends, only using each other discreetly. I am not sure if that worked out or not.

The first day of college, and I am searching for my class, as I am about to enter my appointed class, we bump into each other at the door, where both of our books spread on the floor, and as we both bend down together to pick them up, we bash our heads against each other. “Ouch! That must have hurt!” she says.

And I am like, “Sorry, come again!”

“My head must have hurt you bad! Because I am told I am pretty strong headed, so I thought...”

I burst out laughing so loud, that my laughter roar seemed too embarrassing for everyone present in and around me! I didn’t bother, though. And yet, she blew my mind. Not soon enough I found one of the professors roaring at us, “Get into your class! You think things are funny here?!”

We get inside, I ask her, “Is this your class as well?”

“Of course! Except my name has not been printed outside, yet. But you will definitely find my name printed on these names slip stickers.”

And as she looks down, she sees that the first two books have a different name slips on them. She reads them out, “Who is this P—R—I—Y.... Priya? And what are her books doing with me? My parents named me Mira Rajput!”

Before I can explain to her, she is about to get up and go around asking the class, and I stop her, “Mira, wait, stop. I am Priya. Remember not ten minutes ago we bumped into each other and we dropped our books. They must have mixed up. Relax! You are Mira!”

And we shake on it, laughing it out. That day, it was like we were never the strangers. I found myself blabbering about my school life, my first crush, my teachers, my home and my parents. And surprisingly she did too!

As mentioned earlier, she is Mira Rajput. Yes, belongs to a really 'big family' background. But never showed it, well not intentionally at least! She was pretty down to earth when it came to being her.... especially with me! Her father made his industry from ground to topmost import company. They made some good stationery products. I could make out as she mostly used to have those fancy pens and pencils, with a smooth writing experience. She gifted me many after we became friends. In a way, after meeting her I haven't really had the need to buy extra set of stationery. But since I was always fond of having a bunch of stationery items, thanks to my grandpa. Now that I come to realise it, I think somewhere deep inside, even he was obsessed about having his stock of pencils and erasers and sharpeners and pens and coloured markers. I mean it seemed like he never ran out of them. He hated it when he felt he was running out of black pens or scales. He used to always ask me before going to the big stationery shop that was about 10 minutes away from his home, "Priya bete, is there anything you need from the shop, I have some work around there?"

I used to pretend too to hear him and tease him, as he was too, shit-scared of his wife, as in our grandma, as she used to scream her lungs out, "Suniye, please you really need to stop piling up your stationery items all over your desk and drawers. I have to keep cleaning up your mess, you don't even throw away your old, broken, no-ink pens! I will honestly stop letting you buy anymore!" But in a way, I believe, you all know how most husbands are, they barely listen!

Coming back to my friend, one time, during the second half of the first year itself, as we were attending a class and taking notes, Mira happened to see I was using a different pen, and I cannot exactly explain what got into her, she became a bit possessive. It was a new gel pen by Reynolds, with a click button, and would write smooth. Probably she didn't like the idea of me using another pen or that I was not using her father's pen....as soon as the class was over, she got up and went out. I wasn't sure nor did I realise that she had gone. When I turned to call her, she was not there. I got up and asked a few mates around if they had seen her.... but they all said they didn't. I tried calling her from my Nokia 3310, she kept disconnecting the call. I got worried and straight away went to the canteen, hoping to find her there, she wasn't, then I went to check her on our spot, there she was, sulking.

"What's the matter, M? What just happened? I am a bit confused!"

"Uhhh, Priya.... Look, just know this, I am a bit crazyyy...hope you must be aware by now, and I am also sometimes unpredictable.... possessive...and did I mention I am crazy?! We are friends, and we are beginning to get close, right...and I want us to be friends forever.... but just be aware that I am also possessive about my family. And I know it'd be wrong to say that since you're my friend, you should only be using my father's company pens...I know it's stupidly childish, but I don't know what came over me.... I just got frantic and panicky...I don't know why!!! You will certainly use whatever pen or paper you like...it was wrong of me behaving like that.... just simply know that I just.... I am like that!!! You're going to have to make do with it!! And..."

"Mira, before you say anything further, you should also know this that I am as crazy as you are, as possessive as you....and I am glad we are friends. Just know, I will never leave you hanging nor hurt you. I also know that there will be fights between us, even arguments, but we will make up."

Trrrrrriiiiinnnnnggg goes the bell, and the speaker in the ground goes:

STUDENTS, PLEASE NOTE THAT TODAY DUE TO A SUDDEN INCIDENT, THE COLLEGE SHALL NOT BE TAKING TODAY'S FURTHER CLASSES, UNTIL FURTHER NOTICE. THANK YOU.

The entire college, on hearing this, scream their lungs out, in excitement. Everyone just disperses and it looks like for a moment, there is chaos in the entire college.

And now you all must be wondering about Saket, as I haven't yet mentioned him. Well, not to be too suspicious, this is where Saket comes....in this chaos.

As we are about go to our class to collect our bags and stuff, he comes rushing to us...

"Miya, Piya.... did you listen oo the announcement? I have to come to tell so v 'an o! Looked every ere for you, so came to your class..."

Saket

This boy is one of a kind. He is unusual, sweet, super kind, extremely helpful, always says yes to us, always ready to cook Maggi for us, cause that's what he learnt from his elder brother just before he left for London to study Law a year back. He is also a bit hard of hearing, and his speech is not clear. It's been a birth problem. His family treats him like a normal being, but I feel he is way special for us. He is a brainy kid. It seems like that god took away his hearing, so that he couldn't hear all the nonsense talks happening around, and gave him an Iron man's brain. Like his own family, we too understand him, well, most of the times, sometimes he has to yell or speak really slow, to make us understand. Mira keeps telling him to not yell as that doesn't help in understanding, but that's how he is. He prefers irritating mostly Mira for things she refuses to him for. And he enjoys it! With me, he is gentle, as I feel I wouldn't want to ever hurt him in any way. Could say I have a bit of a soft spot for him.

Vedant and Saket were close too. Saket being the intelligent one, had taught Vedant Math a few times. Vedant being no less a sportsperson, taught Saket how to play cricket and tennis. Bicycling together in the colony, playing together made them pretty close to each other. Saket enjoyed being with them. His parents were mostly out and away, working. And his brother had recently left.

So, whenever he had the chance to come over, he stood with Vedant. They basically understood each other pretty well.

The day the college announced the notice, that day itself it was his idea to go for a picnic...

"Girls, Chalo, let's go for som fun!" He said excitedly.

Mira asked, "Are you planning on taking us for a treat, in your car?"

"Yes, we go in my ca'. You boh' can drive takin' turns. Or le' me drive and you boh' enjoy!

Priya responds immediately before Mira taunts her way to irritate Saket, "Ok Saket, how about you tell us what you have in mind, we can plan accordingly. Then we will all have to inform our parents. And as it is the message must already have reached the parents. How I wish there still were no means to send any message! This is literally becoming the time and age of a new world!"

"Ok, keep your philosophical advice to yourself for now Pri, we have a plan to make and lots to do! So, let's make a move out of here first, go home get changed, inform and pack some snacks." Says Mira, who is all perked up and literally making the moods set.

All three settle in Mira's beetle, and they first head to Mira's. her mother is sitting in the living room with one of her friends. She whisper-calls her mother, *"Mom, can you come here for a minute, please. It's urgent."*

Her mother doesn't understand and raises her hand, signaling her to wait.

Priya walks in behind Mira to look what's taking her so long. As soon as Mira's mom notices Priya, she immediately gets up and comes towards them and asks them softly, "What are you both up to, now?"

Before Mira opens her mouth to talk, Priya utters, "Aunty, we are planning to head to the Gurgaon Mall, the big one. So, we just came to take your permission. We are three of us. Her, myself and Saket, who is waiting in the car. She just came to get her wallet and maybe freshen up. So, do we have your approval?"

"Sure, enjoy yourself. Just be careful and also don't be too late. And no drinking and driving." Mira's mother advises. Then she asks Mira, "Will you be coming home or will you be staying with Priya?"

"I will be staying at her place; hence I will be taking the bag. Thanks, mom!" Replies Mira cheerfully. Then she tells Priya to wait in the car as she will be out in a minute. Priya obliges and offers a polite goodbye to Mira's mom.

"Take care, bachhe." Comes her response.

Priya and Saket are waiting in the car, Mira takes about 10 minutes. She rushes out of her house and yells chirpily, "Next stop.... Saket's?"

Priya laughed softly, responding in a playful tone to match the chirpy outburst. "Well, we both stay close by, so next stop is ours only, honey!"

"Yeah, that's what I meant." Mira says softly.

Traffic makes them reach their house late. Mira rubs her left knee as she says it pains because of the constant use of the clutch and brake. She mentions to Priya, "It's better that we all take turns in driving. I become a bit anxious while driving in this kind of traffic. And plus, we have to go pretty far, so..."

Priya gives a small nod of approval. Priya's mother is in the kitchen taking care of the lunch. "Hello ma! We came to freshen up. We are heading to the big mall in Gurgaon." Priya informs her mother, hesitantly.

"How come you all are home so early? What about your college? Planning to bunk today?" Priya's mother questions her with a hint of sarcasm.

"Well, our college shut down due to some problem, till further notice. We will be informed once they reopen. So, we are going to celebrate today." Mira replies.

Priya goes to her room, Mira follows her, keeps her bag and tells her that she will wait in her car. Priya quickly changes her clothes, splashes her face with cold water and heads out. "Ma, we are leaving." She yells.

"Call up and let your father know." Her mother yells back.

"I will. Bye, ma!" Priya yells, again.

Priya runs towards the car; and notices that Mira is at the back and Saket is in the driver's seat. She motions inquisitively and mouths, "What's going on?"

Mira replies, "For now, he is driving, but on our way back, you can drive. I don't want to drive. And as it is, he said he will drive."

Saket says, "I did. But no' this car. My car. This is tooh girly. I feel weird!"

Priya remarks, "Not fair Mira, you're asking a man to drive a girly car!!" Then she asks Saket, "Are you sure you're ok to drive this, Saket? Or do you want to change to your car?"

Saket replies, "I am ok. Let's go."

Saket decides to take an alternate route to the Gurgaon Mall, hoping to avoid the usual traffic. The journey is relatively smooth, and they reach the mall in decent time. As they approach the parking lot, the sun beats down relentlessly, making the heat almost unbearable. Everyone feels the weight of the scorching rays, growing increasingly desperate to escape into the mall's cool interior.

Reaching the parking entrance, they join a queue of vehicles waiting to drive inside. The slow-moving line tests their patience, but they can't leave Saket alone to handle parking. Finally, after a few more minutes under the blazing sun, they enter the shaded basement parking lot. The relief is immediate as the heavy heat gives way to the cooler, dimly lit space.

The first thing they want to do is, drink lots of water or something cold, so they head to the food court. But not any sooner do they realise that it will take them about half an hour to quench their thirst and hunger. So they go to a restaurant, which is slightly within their budget and decide to pitch in together.

They order straightaway for the main course; some naan and kadhai chicken. And some icy sodas. As soon as their food arrives, they realise, they were really hungry. They gulp down the sodas like it is water. Saket is the only one who eats a bit slowly; he prefers to indulge in it, as he puts it. As decided, they pitch in equally and Mira leaves a tip.

Saket then asks, "Where tooh, now?", like he is the one leading them. Priya initiates, "Let's first go to FabIndia! I've heard here they have the unique clothes."

"Fabindia it is then!" Mira follows. Saket makes a funny face, "Are we here to shop just for you guys?"

"You can shop too, from here, Saket. They have nice kurtas and shirts for boys and men!" Priya tells him. "Ok, good. I need'd some pan's, as i' is..." he responds.

Priya finds herself a nice pair of salwar kameez for herself, she shows it to Mira. Mira is like, "Hmmm.... nice and floral print. Aren't you gonna take a dupatta to go with this?"

"When have you seen me wear a dupatta?! And as it is, it'll become way too expensive, honey! I will just stick with this. What are you buying?" Priya probes.

"I haven't found anything yet. And when have you seen me wear a suit, madam?" Mira snaps. "You go pay for yours and I am heading out." Mira feigns leaving the store but quietly slips behind the shelves, catching the attention of the same associate who had been assisting Priya. She leans in and discreetly requests an identical set to Priya's. By now, Priya has already paid and stepped outside, joining Saket, who is busy sampling different ice cream flavours while she enjoys her cone. Then Mira searches for the matching earrings to be paired with and to gift them to Priya. She thinks she has done good by wanting to twine with her best friend. She tells the associate to keep the bag with them, as she will collect before she leaves.

The associate hesitates, but agrees. She thanks them and walks out, Priya and Saket are looking around searching for Mira. She tip-toes from behind and goes, "BOO!" They both get startled. "Where the heck were you? we've been waiting here, you just disappeared!!" They both literally shriek together. "I was around, just looking. Okay, now what should we explore? There are some more nice stores here...how about Debenhams? This seems like another interesting store."

"No, not that one!" Retorts Priya.

"Okay, then let's go to kiddies store." Mira says, tugging Priya's arm as she led the way with a cheerful bounce in her step.

"Alright, let's go!" Priya agrees, seeing Mira in a cheerful mood. They head to the kiddie's store. On their way to the store, they come across a kiddie toy train, with a man driving it around the mall, with little toddlers and kids, and even grown-up kids, sitting and enjoying the view and waving at the passers-by. Mira jumps in excitement saying, "Let's go in this!! This looks fun!" Priya looks for the starting point of the toy-train, they walk towards that point, and ask the person in-charge. He tells them to wait and hands them a ticket, and asks them to pay Rs.100/- each. They scrunch up their faces after hearing the price, and still want to take a ride. They all become excited and climb the toy train, where it takes them all around the mall. Mira looks at the stores and their names, and keeps talking, "Let's go here, then we'll go here, and we can go look in this store. Oh! This one looks new, we'll go here!" She talks non-stop till the train stops at its usual place. There's a long queue of people waiting with their kids, mostly fathers, whose wives are busy shopping and the dads are busy taking care of their kids, entertaining them and playing with them.

Then they decide to go upstairs and explore some more stores. It's a huge mall, they start to get tired. They realise it when they start dragging themselves around. Saket requests them to head back. Priya immediately agrees, while Mira dramatically pretends to stumble, clutching her forehead. "Can we just go back? Who's driving this time?"

"I'll drive. Let's just go." Priya replies. They start walking towards the elevator from which they came. Saket seems a bit lost, but Priya leads the way. Mira suddenly remembers she left the fabindia bag at the store. "You guys go ahead; I will just come."

"Where are you going now? Will you be able to find your way to the parking lot?" Priya asks concernedly.

"Yeah...I will. I just need to get something and use the washroom. Will not take very long." Mira quickly replies, before the elevator door closes.

They reach the basement and look for the car. They find it, open it and settle in. Now they wait, again! Saket tells Priya, "To'ay was really nice, Priya! I ha' an amazing 'ime. I 'ope we do this again."

"Buddy, we are friends. Of course we will do this again! I had fun too. Best was the train ride, it's like we were little kids again. You remember Appu ghar!

"Yes... I rem'ber! I wen' there wit' my paren's an' my brother. One ticket an' many rides. It was so cool!"

Yeah, right! I went there when I was little with my nani, and then I went there when I was in grade 8th. We had an amazing time! It was a school trip. I loved the merry-go-round with the 'lady and her dress flowing' and then I also remember 'the columbus' boat, swinging back and forth! Wow! Those were really awesome days! I wish to go to Appu ghar again! It brings back so many memories."

"I am surprise' you remember so much, Priya! Let's plan to go again...it migh' refresh your memories." Saket suggests.

"Sounds good. Let's plan. Let Mira come, then we can maybe plan a trip to Appu ghar. I am sure our parents might find it weird or they might just approve willingly. Let's ask and get back on this." Priya responds softly.

Mira takes about 25 minutes to come. "It took you long enough. Did you get lost or something?"

"No baba! Well, yeah, only here in the parking lot. I was about to call you until I realised where you were." Mira replies calmly, but panting away.

"Here, have some water." Priya offers. "What's that in the bag? Did you buy something for yourself from fabindia?" She asks enthusiastically.

"Well, drive first, let's get out of here, it's already 8pm. We will be scolded if we reach so late! Someone's going to throw a fit." Mira changes the conversation.

Saket offers Mira to sit in the front, but she refuses and chooses to sit comfortably at the back with her legs folded. They pay for the parking at the exit and head back. It nearly takes them an hour to reach because of heavy traffic. But then they feel it was a 'memorable and a joyous day'. They all have smiles on their faces. Saket wants to ask about their trip to Appu ghar, but then he just drops the idea and leaves it for another day.

Priya steps out of the car, and tells Saket, "It was fun having you with us." Mira yells from inside the car, "I second that, Saket. I had fun too! Especially the train ride. That's a moment and now a memory to be cherished! See you later, buddy! Take care and goodnight!"

Saket feels touched. And he walks back home. Mira and Priya head inside, greet the parents and head to Priya's room. They both dump their paper bags on the floor, near the cupboard, and Priya heads to the bathroom, quickly splashes her face with cold water, changes and comes out. Mira lets her know, "Your brother came and asked about their dinner."

Priya replies, "I am not really that hungry. What about you...what did you say?"

"I just told him we are coming. What was I supposed to say?" Mira responds calmly.

"Okay, then let's go. Although I am way too tired to eat." Priya sighs.

"Let's eat and sleep." Mira encourages Priya.

They drag themselves to the dining table, eat slowly. When they're done, they put their plates in the sink, and bid goodnight to the parents and head back to the room. Priya turns off the lights, Mira is in the mood to discuss about the day, but Priya tells her to sleep. Mira turns to the other side and conks off. They both do.

* * * * *

CHAPTER 4

Meet Sameer!

"Once in a lifetime, you meet someone who changes everything!"

Next morning, around 7 am, Priya is awoken with some noise. As she steps out, she hears an argument going on between her mother and her brother about taking a tiffin. Even though he is a big foodie, but he refuses to take something from home. It is not 'COOL', according to him. He only prefers to go to a canteen and have samosas and patties or pastries. God only knows how hygienic it would be! But then, I also like to do it. Anyways, their argument is ended when I enter. Mom being a mom, packs a tiffin for my brother and hands it over to him saying, "Eat it. Don't dump it". He walks off sulking and mumbling.

Priya heads back to her room to get ready to go to college, as she enters, she sees Mira almost awake. To trouble her, she makes a gesture to jump on her, but then gives up thinking it would seem odd. But still feeling naughty, throws a pillow on her face and pulls her blanket off. "I'm up you moron!" screams Mira.

"I am not a moron, you are! Fine, I won't play with you, lets' just get ready we have to go!" Priya frowns.

"Awwwww, someone's sulking!" says Mira.

"Look, I am going to go get ready, you can get ready after me! Says Priya in a commanding tone.

"Yeah, go ahead. Till then I'll plan our day. Ok?" asks Mira.

"Whatever. Just don't make a dumb plan." Replies Priya and closes the door behind her.

Meanwhile, Mira decides to surprise Priya in order to make her have a good day, she texts Sameer.

"Hi, rem'br me?" And awaits his reply.

Her mobile goes 'tiiing'. She looks at the reply and it reads, "yes. Hru?"

"Let's meet. Venue will msg." texts Mira.

After about 5 minutes comes the reply, "k".

Feeling super excited, thinking she has done something marvellously great, tries to sit still, but isn't able to. So, she goes to knock on Priya's bathroom door, but ends up excitedly banging on it.

"Coming dude!" comes Priya's response.

Mira doesn't want Priya to become too suspicious so she tries to calm herself by taking a few deep breaths. And just then, Priya comes out, smelling all floral and looking fresh, her shoulder length hair, wet as she probably shampooed, comes out wearing her recently gifted Fabindia's semi-patiala salwar with an ajrakh print kurta. It is pretty much in vogue. She always wanted to get something from here, as she posed. She loved the brand. It has simple ethnic clothes for men and women. In a pretended voice, Mira asks, "Dude, why on earth are you dressed in an Indian attire?"

Priya seems stumped by this reaction from Mira, but replies in a casual way, "Dude, coz I wanted to wear it today! I feel good and plus it's new and my favourite...and I feel comfortable as well."

"Does this mean that I am supposed to twine with you, then?" Mira asks anxiously.

"Why are you asking these kinds of questions, M? What's gotten into you suddenly? It's completely up to you. And by the way I haven't really seen you in an Indian attire, so maybe you could show me, you know! And bt dubbs, what do you mean by 'twine'? Do you have the same combination like mine?" Priya is perplexed.

"Well, dearie, if you remember correctly, who chose these in the first place, I bought it for you and suggested that we both should have these, so I went ahead and bought for myself as well. And I have a small surprise for you. Just be completely ready, comb your hair and everything and I'll be back in a jiffy." Mira steps into the bathroom, taking her phone along, making sure Priya doesn't notice it. But Priya does, she prefers to not react to it as she has a lot to take in to what just happened.

Mira doesn't take too long in coming out. She comes out in the same salwar-suit as Priya's. When they both look at each other, they just shake their heads and Mira grabs her bag and takes out a pair of jeans and a checked linen shirt, rushes in the bathroom and changes. In the meantime, Priya is grabbing her box full of funky earrings, and looking to find the one to match with her outfit. Mira, who is aware about Priya, soon after changing, takes out a small pouch from her bag, and hands it over to Priya, "Leave your box and keep it aside, take these and try them on."

"What are these? Where did you get them? Mira!!!! What.... I am stunned!! What is into you today?! You're really making me anxious today.... what has gotten into you all of a sudden?! There's something going on...and you're not telling me...are you trying to fix me up...or my mom has got to you as well? Just tell me!"

"First of all, Pri, just a 'thank you' would suffice. And secondly, there is nothing going on. Can't I just gift my friend something? I liked it so I bought it. There's nothing to get anxious about. And finally, your mom has not got to me, I am just celebrating our friendship. Is that too much?" Says Mira, trying to make Priya calm down.

Priya opens the pouch and finds pretty little Jhumki's. Her eyes get a bit teary and she puts them on. They match well with her suit. Mira who has gone to comb her hair in the bathroom, comes out and when she looks at Priya all set and looking her prettiest, hugs her and says, "I am so glad we are friends, and now can we go? We are getting late. And there is a dim chance that a message is going to go across our parents and this time my father is certainly going to throw a fit at me...so please let's just leave now!" Mira sounds super agitated.

Priya thinks to herself, Mira is either worried about something or she is hiding something. She just behaves casually and says, "I am ready, let's go."

And they head out taking their tiffin and bags. To make the aura calmer, and sitting in the car, Priya asks Mira, "By the way babe, where and how did you manage to choose my outfit? I mean we went together, as far as I remember."

"What are you trying to ask, P?"

"I am asking where was I when you chose this for me?" asks Priya pointing to her outfit while sitting and getting comfortable and fastening her seat belt.

Mira looks at Priya sternly and says, "You and Saket were busy buying an ice cream, you dummy!!" She starts the car and drives.

Priya is left speechless. She suddenly remembers that it was only yesterday, when they all went shopping during the college shut down. For a moment it feels like it was days ago. They were supposed to go for a long drive but instead ended up going to the Gurgaon mall.

Priya is so lost in her thoughts that she doesn't even realise that they have reached their college. Mira is finding her parking spot, and Priya is reaching out in the back seat to grab the bags. As she grabs her own bag, the tiffin box rolls down and the Tupperware cover opens, probably because it was not properly closed. "Oops!" goes Priya.

"What 'oops? What's wrong, P?" Mira sounds harsh.

"Nothing, just dropped my tiffin. The sandwich fell out." Says Priya in a normal tone.

"P, I hope nothing was soiled. I love my car inside out. You know I dislike any stale smell or any kind of dirt in my car. Please be careful."

Priya steps out and gives a stern look to Mira and says, "Mira Rajput, I am completely aware that you love your car, and the sandwich was baked, it did not soil your seat nor your floor mat. But instead of asking what I will eat now, you are mostly concerned about your car! And even if it was dirty, you could get your car cleaned 'inside & out'. But this sandwich was only cooked by my mom for you and for me." She hands over Mira's bag to her and takes her own and walks away.

Suddenly Mira's phone starts ringing. It's Sameer. Mira remembers she was planning to make Sameer and Priya meet. She forgets about the recent scenario and picks up his call.

"Hey Neighbour! What's happening?"

"What do you mean 'what's happening'? You asked me meet you but never told me the place or time...so I am only confirming. Why did you ask me to meet you? Is everything ok? Are you in trouble or something?" Sameer asks all these questions in his husky-manly voice. He sounds concerned, to which Mira sparks a plan in her mind. And tells Sameer to come to their college. He agrees.

Mira heads to the class, and reaches just as the bell rings. She goes and sits next to Priya, coz that is her place. Priya has tears in her eyes. Mira for the time being, ignores her tears and listens to the lecture, makes a few notes. The lecture gets over, Priya keeps sitting in her seat, doesn't look at Mira nor does she talk.

Mira texts her. "I am sorry for being so harsh out there, P. we have one important class, then let's go have lunch, my treat. Please forgive me."

Priya looks at her phone. Starts to type, but doesn't. But then she forgives and forgets and types in "Fine."

Mira is relieved. And they smile at each other wait for the next teacher to come. Now they can't wait to head out. And Mira has a plan of her own. Unfortunately, their teacher was on leave. They receive the message from the other professor who comes to announce in their class. Mira doesn't miss the chance to text Sameer saying that their class was cancelled. So, he should reach the venue before them.

"Done." Comes his reply.

Mira tells Priya, "Hey P, since the class isn't happening, how about we go for the treat I promised you!"

"Alright. Let's go. Where have you thought we go?"

"Depends on what you want to have."

"Do we have any options or choices?"

"Well, since it's completely up to me, then just sit and go with me on this. Let's enjoy."

"Alright. Whatevs."

And they head back to their car and drive to the destination-Sameer!

Meanwhile, Sameer reaches the venue which is.... (Drum rolls, please) 'Drumsticks in CP'. It is one of the happening places in Delhi. As mentioned, prior, with the Delhi traffic, it takes them about 30 minutes to reach the place. Whereas Sameer reaches in 15 minutes, being on his Bullett. Mira manages to get the perfect parking spot, which seemed surprising. Priya heads out and helps Mira park her car properly. They both enter the Café cum bar cum restaurant. Sameer has already ordered himself a beer. And he's sitting upstairs. Some great music is playing and Mira looks for Sameer and takes out her phone to text and ask him.

Before she can type, he texts her, "Look up, silly."

She looks up and waves at him. She calls aloud to Priya and signals her to come up. Priya follows her.

"Hey ladies! You made it in good time."

Priya stops fiddling with her bag and is stunned to hear the voice. She just Frozzzeeee. It suddenly strikes her and she remembers that husky-manly voice. At that very moment she feels she has lost all power to speak or move. She looks up from behind Mira and sees him.

"Hey! Good to see you here. Were you following us? Or were we following you?" Mira is still pretending. But Sameer goes with the flow, unable to understand the situation. Priya is still staring at him; she cannot get over the fact that he is right in front of her.

"Hey P, meet Sameer, officially! Let's sit here only... hope you don't mind."

Priya just shakes her head and gives a thumbs up. She still finds herself to be speechless. Though she has millions of thoughts and questions running in her mind. *'What is he doing here? How did he manage to follow us yet reach before us? Am I looking weird...am I being obnoxious...How am I supposed to behave? Why am I feeling so shy? This is not how it's supposed to be! He's not my boyfriend.... Why is it that I can hear my thoughts so loud...this has never happened before! I hope nobody can hear my thoughts or see the bubbles popping out of my head!! God.... this is so bizarre!!!!*

"Hey Priya, nice to meet you, 'officially'!

"Likewise. Can I get a second with Mira? We'll be right back." And saying this Priya takes her out of his sight, kind of.

"Dude, what are we doing here? Do you know I can literally hear my thoughts screaming away at me! What the hell is he doing here? How did he know we will be here...? And I have no clue what to talk or say... I am absolutely blank here! Please help me out." Blabbers Priya in a single breath. Well, almost.

"Relax Priya, take a breath. Do you remember in the café you told me you had a crush on this guy? Well, here he is. Now you can guesstimate if he is your crush or your infatuation or the love of your life! It's simple baby!!"

Priya is taken aback! She is not sure what to say to this reply. "Are you seriously setting me up? Have you lost your mind? Well, in a way, yes, I like him. He is nice and quite good looking and....and I am out of words. Mira Rajput, if it'd had been someone else or if I find out that you and my mom are together on this... I swear I am going to throw you in the dumpster. For now, let's head back inside else that poor fellow is going to think we left him hanging, despite you inviting him."

Mira looks at Priya guiltily. Priya pats on her back gently and they both head back to where Sameer's sitting.

"Welcome back again ladies." Showing some chivalrousness, he gets up and lets them both sit, raises his hand to call the bartender. "What'll you both have?"

"I'll have a red wine. I am not sure about her..." Mira's cut short and Priya conveys to the bartender that she'll have a Bacardi breezer-cranberry.

"Nice one, bro!" reacts Mira. "I believe this is your first time?"

"You still don't know many things about me, M! Let's just enjoy for now." Priya speaks softly. And she feels nice about his civilized behaviour. She can still hear her thoughts loud and clear, *'Didn't know there are guys with chivalry. He seems like a charming gentleman, has a good vibe around him. But the big question is, will we ever be together, and if we are, will we survive together?? Ugh!!!.... this needs to stop! Seriously, this brain of mine needs to stop!!Just focus, P. Live in the now. Don't think too much. Take a few deep breaths and calm yourself. Stop panicking. Just go with the flow. Don't overwhelm yourself. There's a long way ahead. Relax and enjoy.'*

Priya comes back to the present situation where Mira and Sameer are busy talking about college and he is sharing his days soon after he finished his studies and how his father sent him to London for business studies as he wanted his son to join his business. Priya is gawking at him like he is some celebrity. She is being quite attentive to his conversations. She is just amazed at his personality. She tries really hard for her thoughts to not come in between.

"So, what about you Priya? What are you doing? What are your thoughts and opinions about your future? Would like to share?" Inquires Sameer.

"Well, honestly, I haven't really given it a deep thought. I am just focussing on performing well in my current course which is in Arts, then probably I will decide what I wish to pursue. I am simply going with the flow." Replies Priya in a very calm manner.

Mira seems impressed and taps on her thigh and mouths, "Way to go, babe!"

Sameer has a pleased look. He smiles and says, "Okay. So basically, you are a content girl who knows what she is doing?"

“Is that a question? Asks Priya.

“I am just getting to know you. We are being friends, right? I somewhat know Mira, as you must be aware we are neighbours, right? And her mom and my mom are really good friends. I call them ‘the sugar’ friends...” Sameer is cut short when Priya and Mira both pitch in and ask, “What does ‘the sugar’ friends mean? What is the story to that?”

Sameer becomes conscious for a second and then replies, “Well, you know, like one lady goes to the new neighbour’s house with an idea to get some sugar but with an intention to see the inside of the house and of course be acquainted. That is what I meant. And this is how they met. But don’t ask me who went to whose house, please!”

And they both laugh out loud. Priya realises that the aura of them being together has taken off with a good start. She quietly touches the wooden table in front of her and thanks her stars for giving her the friends she never had before. Soon, their table is filled with different varieties of breads and pizzas and noodles.

Just when it’s time to go, Mira offers to pay as she says she had promised Priya it’s her treat. Sameer stops her and says, “I believe we are meeting first time, officially and this is our first day to being friends. So, let me pay for today, you can give her a treat some other day, since you both meet every day. So, yeah.”

Mira doesn’t argue too much as they had stuffed themselves so much that they didn’t have the strength. Priya watches Sameer swipe his card. She is in complete awe of him. They all head out and Sameer takes Mira aside. Priya gasps. They both whisper something to each other and Mira comes back to Priya, unlocks the car and tells Priya to sit. Priya stares at Mira, "Would you want me to ask you or are you going to tell on your own what that was?"

Mira looks at Priya and gets a curious vibe. "Ok, chillax baby. Since you are aware that I you have a liking to him. He was .... look..." Mira is a bit hesitant. But she starts to think of what she can tell her. Finally, she just spurts out, "He too likes you, ok...there I said it!"

Priya gets flabbergasted and retorts, "I never meant for you to say that, M! And I am pretty sure that is not what he said. It must have been something else. And plus, he himself said that this is the beginning of our new friendship. So quit lying and it's ok if you don't want to share. I shouldn't have asked in the first place. So, you 'chillax' and tell me what your plan is for tonight...as I am really hoping you stay with me for a few more days. And as it is our exams are round the corner. How about we forget about everything else and start preparing?"

"Guess you're right, Priya! But for tonight I have to go back home. My father texted me and wanted to see me. Then he travels again form day after. So, for now, I'll go drop you, take my stuff and will see when I do!"

Priya asks, "But you'll be coming to college, na? Don't skip college, please."

"Of course not. I have to be with you. Else you'll go mad, without me!!" Smiles Mira.

Priya feels a sense of sadness and anger. She feels Mira is hiding something and fears that they are suddenly falling apart. Lately, they have been fighting and arguing a lot. Somewhere, Priya feels she needs to control her anger and get herself to calm down. She also realises she is becoming hyper, probably because her life is changing, somehow. She can't figure it out. Right now, she just perceives that she is simply tired and wants to relax for a day. Sit and think everything over. Spend time with her family. And then restart. (Sometimes we all need that, right!)

As Priya enters her home, literally dragging herself inside, takes a glass of water and sees her father sitting in the living room with a book and a cup of coffee. "Had a good and a fruitful day, today bete? You look tired. Should I make you some tea or coffee?" He asks in a loving way.

"No, papa. I am ok. Just needed a glass of water, is all."

The living and dining are a mutual room with an open kitchen for easy access. It was designed this way. It was my father's idea to have it this way so that whenever mom would cook, she wouldn't feel too lonely. He also made sure that he got a small space made for her to place the radio. She felt comforted while cooking and listening to the radio. My father mostly cared about everyone, but himself.

* * * * *

CHAPTER 5

My Father – My Strength

"My father gave me the greatest gift anyone could ever give; he believed in me"
"A father doesn't tell you he loves you. He shows you."

"Priya, I suggest you go and take a short nap for a while. You honestly look tired. You have to rest; your exams are nearing. You need to be mentally relaxed to attempt them."

"But papa, if I sleep now, I won't be able to sleep at night, and I cannot disturb my sleep at night!" Groans Priya.

"I will wake you up in half an hour, I promise."

"No. I don't want that either. Can't I just sit here with you?" Pleads Priya to her father.

"Yes, you may." And he gets back to his book. While Priya finds a 3-seater couch, goes to it and plops down. Within minutes she dozes off.

A little while later, the doorbell rings, and it's the mailman. Hearing the bell, Priya wakes up with a startle. Papa takes the mail and gestures at Priya telling her to go back to sleep. This time, realising that her eyes are still drowsy, she lays back down and sleeps.

Usually when this happens, people tend to lose their sleep, the second time.

I am pretty sure you must have faced this issue. The simple solution to that would be, to make your head become absolutely blank. Trust me, it works. It'll take an effort, but it'll certainly work. Stop thinking. Tell your brain to stop.

In the background, sub-consciously Priya keeps hearing some sounds like cups clashing, people talking, papers rustling. She opens her eyes and sees her father holding another cup, but he is bringing it to her. "Here's your tea, Gudiya!"

"Thank you, papa. But you didn't have to." Groans Priya, still sounding sleepy.

"I told you I would wake you. I will let mummy know you're awake. We'll all sit here in the living room. She also just woke up." Says her father matter of factly.

Priya sits and wonders how much she is loved by her father, who has always tried to support her. Her mother has been her emotional and mental support. Yet, she feels incomplete and discontent somewhere. She feels she has left some bad memories in her mind and haven't replaced them with the fresh and good ones. Like for example, she just met Sameer. And she has good friends like Saket and Mira. And suddenly it strikes her that she has just had a misconception, probably with Mira. And she needs to clear that. But as of now, all that matters is that she wants her parents by her side. She cannot remember the last time they all sat together to have a cup of tea, in the living room. Her mother calls for her brother, Vedant. He comes dragging his feet, and everyone goes, "Stooooop! Don't do that. It's annoying!" He gives a devilish smile.

So, everyone sits on their favourite spots, get comfortable, with their special mugs. Vedant has a cold coffee mug, mom, papa and Priya have chai mugs. And while everyone is relishing their teas and coffees, Priya's father suggests they discuss about their lives. Priya feels her father seems aware that something is bothering her, and is not being able to say it. So, he announces that everyone opens up about themselves.

"I'll go first, since I am the youngest." Says Vedant, always sounding mischievous. The father tells Vedant to go ahead. "I don't have much to say except I have been selected in the cricket team this time as a batsman. Our coach wants us to be at school at 7 am every day, so starting tomorrow, I start my training. And my buddy Anubhav is also a part, so we are together in it."

"Wow, that is some great news, beta!" Says papa excitedly. Mom suddenly asks, "And what time do you think you'll be coming home on practice days?"

"I think between 3:30 and 4 pm. I will have to confirm, ma."

"Enjoy, beta. As long as we know your studies are not suffering. We just don't want you failing your tests." Warns papa. Even though everyone knew that Vedant was a go-getter. He was a brilliant kid, with a genius mind and he was certainly hard working. Getting selected in the cricket team seemed like his dream come true. So, everyone was really happy. They all cheered for Vedant and clanked their mugs together. Next turn was taken by Papa, which he announced, even though he said he would take last. But before he could start, mom called out and said aloud, "I have been asked to be the Principal of Gurukul School. I haven't yet replied to them. But it came as a surprise to me, but a college friend got in touch with me after ages, and she has her own school, and she wants me join. I am overwhelmed. I have no idea what to say. Will I be able to do it?"

Everyone could see mom was getting anxious, but then, we were a family, we supported each other. We were each other's support and strength. We all cheered for mom, telling her it was ok, and she could manage very well. So, she could say yes to her friend. And she would start asap. Priya and Vedant hugged their mom. And Vedant suddenly exclaimed, "So, this is why you have been screaming at me, because you were overwhelmed and couldn't decide!"

And Priya bumps him on his head, giving him the dirtiest look. And he's like, "Whaaaaat?!?! What did I say?!"

Papa interrupts them, "Ok Priya, you want to share something now?"

"Not really, papa! I am fine. I just wanted this together time, is all."

"You know you can share whatever you're feeling right now. We are here for you." Says mom softly.

Papa holds mom's hand telling her to let it be. And he gives Priya a look which tells her that it's ok if she doesn't feel like sharing now, she can let it go. He is there. He'll make things better.

Priya lets out a sigh. And soon papa announces that he is the head of his department, and that he'll be taking care of extreme cases along with dividing or segregating the doctors to different fields. He too seemed enthusiastic about it. Every one cheers for papa, and the chai-mugs are empty this time, yet, they all come close and hug altogether. Priya in her mind feels left out, and she hates this feeling of being left out. She realises she has been trying to control her tears, but is unable to. She rushes to her bedroom quietly and closes the door behind her. She steps into the washroom and splashes water on her face, trying once again to hold back her tears. This time, however, they flow freely, uncontrollably, like water from a broken faucet. She feels so low that she has let everyone down by not achieving anything. She looks at herself in the mirror and says, "I will become a much better person and achieve my goal, because I can!"

Suddenly there is a knock on the door. "Priya, bete, can I come in?"

It's papa. She quickly wipes her face and opens the door. "Hi papa!"

"Sweetheart, what is the matter? You have to share your feelings. If you keep them inside, you will not be happy. It'll keep loading up and one day you will find yourself to be really discontent, aloof and unhappy. We wouldn't want that ever for you. Your mom and I, we are really proud of you. And we have been discussing that there is something eating you up from the inside since quite some time. So, tell me or tell mom. Did something bad happen to you?

Priya says, "No, not at all, papa."

"Then, did you have a fight with Mira?" Enquired her father.

"No, well. It wasn't a fight. But I guess a misunderstanding, you could say. Or rather, not her fault entirely but somewhat my fault too. And mostly, I have been kind of agitated." Replies Priya.

"You want me to call mummy here. Would you like to share your thoughts with her? She might be able to guide you better." Her father tries to ease it out for her.

"Papa, I know that I am a laid-back person, I haven't achieved anything amongst all of us. I also know that.... I have come this far. You remember in school days; I never had any close friends. I was always desperate to get friends. Finally, when I entered college, I found Mira. And of course, Saket. I feel that I must have done something right in life to get these kinds of friends. I have you, mom & Vedant. I have this beautiful room of mine. I know and understand it means that I must be deserving it. I am doing something right. But, still why do I feel so low and frustrated all the time, I am not being able to figure. I adore Mira, but sometimes she also does things which are not right. I have been a good student, and I love what I am learning. I have no intentions of getting married. At last, I'm learning to appreciate my life and make the most of every moment. I didn't want to be a doctor, but I know you wanted one of us to follow in your footsteps. I know we have a complete freedom to choose for ourselves. I know I have a heart like you. You love unconditionally. But just understand, papa. I am still in my learning phase. I am still organizing my life accordingly. You all have everything figured out. You are a father. Just trust me. I know I have yours and mom's complete support. I will not let you down. All I want is for you to be there mentally and physically, papa. I will sort things out myself when I know I have you all by my side. You are my strength, papa." While saying this, both Priya and her father have tears in their eyes. Her father kisses her on her forehead, hugs her and assures her that **he will always be there**.

"Priya, we love you a lot. And now I believe you should give Mira a call. She will feel nice. Talk things out with her. If you don't clear the air, things might escalate into a big issue. And I haven't seen Saket, call him as well. You guys are "the triplets". Don't let yourselves break into a million pieces." States papa. Priya responds with a smile. But before she decides to call her friends, she takes out her diary and starts to jot her thoughts down.

Dear Diary,

I believe I can now say that today turned out to be a fruitful day, coz it is going to end well. I started to have a pleasant day, till things got ruined by me. But then for some time, I forgot about everything else and met Sameer.

Although I cannot say much about him yet, but he seems courteous. He is not just handsome, but he is charming, compassionate and considerate. I really wonder if I am his type. Regardless of that, I was told by Mira that he could be into me. He mustn't be too older than me. He said he just started with his father's business. He has done business studies from London. That also means he is quite intelligent. Nevertheless, I think I shouldn't really worry about that as I am sure, if he is destined to be mine, then nothing can stop us and if not, then I could probably think of trying but if I fail, then God help me. I will focus on my goal....

Also, today, I let my heart out to my father. It feels really good from inside. I know in my heart that I shared what I was supposed to, rest only I have to figure out what is to be done. Call it guilt or truth, but I have never felt this low because today also was 'an achievement day' for everyone but me. My parents and my brother achieved something they have been wanting. I, on the other hand, not much. But according to my father, I have achieved as much. Why doesn't it feel so?

Till next time!

Priya sets down her diary and avoids undergoing the same feeling. So, she picks up her phone and starts to message Saket. "Heyy bud, whts hap'g?"

"Noth'g mch, u tell." Comes his reply

"Wanna hangout?" types in Priya.

"Now?" Responds Saket.

"Sure." Texts Priya.

* * * * *

CHAPTER 6

'I Am Sorry, Mira!'

"It's never too late to make things right."

Within 10 minutes or so, the doorbell rings, and he greets her parents. Her father knocks on the door, "Priya, Saket is here."

"Come in, papa. I called & invited him." Yells Priya.

Her father opens the door, lets Saket in, and he gives Priya the look like he is appreciating her. Saket enters and immediately bombards her with questions. "Where th' heck did you disappear to? No call, no message. I only met your parents a few times, but you...? I 'ven't seen Mira either. Is everything alright be'ween you two? Why are you lookin' like you 'ave murdered someone?"

"Shhhhhhhhh Saket! Calm down buddy! What's with so many questions, dude?! I am right here, aren't I? I never disappeared. And I texted you tonight, and invited you here to talk, right?! Well, you know you are a few houses away from ours, you could have also called or messaged or dropped in!? Look I have not called you here so we could argue. Not with you too!"

"Wha' duz that mean, Pri?"

"Look, in simple words. I screwed up, alright. Now I want to and have to make things right." Priya sounds jittery.

"Let me guess. You don't want to go into 'oo many details, am I right?" Saket sounds sarcastic.

"Something like that. I will explain everything later. Right now, can you just help me, please?"

"You never have to ask, Pri. But you also said that you called me here to talk. So, talk! You have to give me something, else I will not be able to help." Claims Saket.

"Fair enough." Priya responds. And she explains everything to Saket.

After it is understood by him, he jumps up and declares that they go to her place and she can explain to her. And clear the air!

Priya yells and says, "Dude, it's late. I will not be allowed to go now! I can simply text her now or maybe in the morning. I just wanted to let you know and I was maybe hoping that you could help me. And in a way I owe you too an apology, for not being in contact and not keeping you in the loop."

"Awwww P, it's ok. Don't feel sorry. You're going 'oo make me cry! I am a gud friend. Alvays here for you and Mira."

As they are talking, Priya's mom brings them some maggi and juice. Vedant follows his mom, only to get a bite out of his sister's bowl. He hides as his mom enters Priya's room. Priya avoids drinking too much of soft drinks and neither does she prefer to serve any to her friends. Her parents oblige with her decision. And on the other hand, Vedant being the naughtiest brat, always did what was not allowed. Although he did understand its side effects, so he didn't take it too often. He mostly wanted to tease his sister.

Coming back, Saket takes his bowl, smells the aroma, and keeps it aside only to let it cool. Priya takes the bowl and she also keeps it aside, Vedant, quickly grabs the bowl, takes a big bite and runs off screaming, "HOT, HOT, HOT!!! I BURNT MY TONGUE!!!" Priya yells at him, "Silly boy, why do you think I kept it away, Vedu, you are seriously something!!"

He yells back, "I only thought you were letting me have it…how was I to know…"

"You perfectly knew, don't act so dumb!" Replies Priya in the same tone as his.

Saket sits and giggles. He knows how Priya and Vedant argue and patch up soon enough. He admires their affection towards each other, as he hasn't seen that much of love, respect and affection between many siblings. Some only get mature and understand. Finally, he picks up the bowl, and asks, "Now how do you want to tackle your situation? How do you plan to approach Mira and clear the air?"

Priya is absolutely flabbergasted. For a moment there, she completely forgot about it. She hated being reminded of something she wanted to procrastinate. But then she only thought this was necessary. She had a night to think it over and validate. They both finish their soupy noodles, slurping it away and Saket is busy taking each bite carefully so it doesn't finish off quickly. Priya too enjoys her bowl of noodles, but she is usually quick in everything, so she manages to finish it off before Saket. Though it's late, Priya tells Saket to go home and meet her in the morning after she texts him. He obliges and takes his bowl, offers to take hers as well, but she refuses and goes with him to keep it in the kitchen so she could see him off. He has a tendency that sometimes if he is not told to leave, he could stay for hours at a stretch. He has sometimes done it with Vedant, when they have played video games with each other. But then, he understood and said goodnight and goodbye to Priya, waved at her father and went off. Priya found her father sitting at his usual place, this time watching TV. He mostly watched English movies. In those days, there were many interesting movies coming on the dish tv. Papa's most favourite was 'Scent of a Woman and Godfather trilogy. These movies he loved to watch whenever they were aired on TV, which was almost every time he turned on the TV. He either would hold on to mom or me or Vedant. Vedant used to escape away making funny excuses, like he had to use the washroom or things like that. Mom would get away by saying, "NOT AGAIN!" and Priya would get stuck sometimes. She used to run out of excuses, so she would sit with him to watch 'Scent of a Woman'. It was a brilliant movie. And a few times he tried to make her watch Godfather, which Priya found a bit boring. It was only due to her father that she got used to watching action genre movies. She enjoyed rom-coms as well, but since Priya's mind was constantly running with things, she believed is why I enjoyed myself with her father. They were both somewhat alike. She smiles and sits with her father saying, "I'll sit with you for a while, then I'll go and sleep." He seems happy with her thought and smiles at her.

Next morning, after she wakes up, finishes up with her morning routine, she picks up her phone to give Saket a reminder about the day, but instead she sees tons of messages on her mobile. Some are from Mira and some from Saket and one from Sameer. She gets thrilled to see that she received a message from him. But is surprised to see Mira's message. Before she starts to read the message, she gets a call on her landline. Her mother picks up from the other room. She immediately calls out, "Priya, it's Mira, please pick up."

"I have picked up, ma. Thanks. Hello...Mira! How are you? I was about to call you today and planned to meet you. Can we talk? I...." Priya responds sounding worried and desperate.

"I know, P. Saket called me up in the morning and told me everything. Look, I wasn't aware that you went in so deep regarding a small thing. We just had some miscommunication, a misunderstanding. That's all. Just relax. Let's meet, I am going to a salon, can you come there or should I pick you up?"

"Which salon are you talking about? The one in the mall or the one close to your place, which one?" Priya interrogates.

"I am coming to pick you up, get ready if you're not." Commands Mira.

"OK." And before Priya can say anything, the call is disconnected.

Priya goes to her mother and lets her know that she will be going to a salon with Mira. Her mother seems absolutely cool about it and tells her to take some money if she plans to get anything done. She doesn't say anything else.

Priya goes back to her room and takes out her most comfortable loose clothes, and decides in her mind what to get done and what all to talk to her. Suddenly she remembers that she'd received a message from Sameer. She immediately grabs her phone and reads the message. It says,

"It was nice to meet you the other day. I came to know you have a sort of liking towards me. I am flattered. Would you like to meet up for coffee sometime? Your choice of place."

She is thrilled to see the message and forgets all about everything else for the moment. She thinks how is it that he messaged out of the blue after the other day! She believed she didn't make much of an impression with him and maybe she was a bit clumsy. After meeting him, she thought that he was completely out of her league, and he would like to date someone his age. She wore a suit, for Christ's sake! She wasn't even aware that Mira was going to schedule a meeting with him!

Then it makes her ponder that Mira should have just hinted her about it. So much of thinking makes her have a headache again, on the same side. She feels her head has started to throb.

Anyhow, she looks at the time and quickly rushes to have a shower and get ready before Mira comes. While she gets ready, she decides to take a medicine after and craves for a nice cup of tea or strong coffee. She steps out and there's the honking of her car. Priya's mom yells from her bedroom, "Priya, probably Mira's here. Are you ready yet?"

"Haan ma! I'll let her know I'll be out in 5 minutes." Yells back Priya.

Priya calls her from the landline. "Mira, give me 2 minutes. I'm coming."

She has to lie to her about the 2 minutes as she doesn't want her to know about her chai craving or the headache. She quickly grabs her box of medicines, takes out the pain killer and gobbles it down with water kept on her bedside table. And she takes her bag and hurries out.

"Ma, I am leaving." Yells Priya.

Her mom doesn't reply as she knows. Priya rushes out to Mira who is waiting in her car, adjusting her rear view. "Hi!" Says Priya.

"How are you doing?" asks Mira.

"All good. Where are we going?

"So, I was thinking that let's make today as our day. As in 'we get pampered day'! where we get ourselves face cleansed, and manicured and pedicured and massaged, and hair all shiny and spa'd! Also, maybe we can order some coffee or chai with some sandwich or a pizza!"

"Wow! Sounds good and someone's in the mood! All ok with you, M? Enquires Priya.

"Yeah! I am absolutely fine. Why do you ask? Probes Mira.

"No. It's just.... we haven't talked for a few days. And I was wondering how.... you know. I am really sorry, Mira! I really, truly am! Whatever was the misunderstanding, or a miscommunication between us, I hope it doesn't happen again. Also, it would be nice that you shared whatever is in your mind or heart that you plan to do for me. It'll only make me happy if you're planning a pleasant surprise for me, or whatever. Just let me know. Can you please do that?" Priya is almost in tears.

Mira's eyes, filled with tears, haven't looked to the road; she hasn't started to drive yet. She comes closer to Priya and hugs her. "I am sorry too, P! I won't hurt you anymore. You're my good and close friend. Let's be more communicative from now on. And you-stop taking everything to heart, ok?! You are so bold and yet, you behave like a little girl, you know that?!"

"I am not! But my father always says that we should always keep our inner child alive at all times. That way, we don't grow old very fast and we feel young even after we grow old." States Priya wiping her tears away. She also feels her headache is going away; she was glad to have taken the medicine.

"Shall we move? Did you take an appointment or something?" Beseeches Priya.

"Yeah, when you called earlier, I had just taken an appointment from them." Acknowledges Mira.

And they drive up to a place in Hauz Khas. The place looks huge; it's a triple storeyed building and a unisex salon- 'Toni & Luxe'. As they enter, they are welcomed with an apple drink. Then a lady at the reception asks them if they have an appointment. Mira comes forward and says she took an appointment nearly an hour ago for 2 people.

The receptionist with an accent asks, "By which name did you make an appointment?"

Mira responds, "I took an appointment under my name, Mira Rajput."

"Ok, did you specify what all you'll be getting done?" She asks again.

"Madam, I simply took an appointment, saying I will see what I will get done, depending on the time taken. Can you just check if there is an appointment under this name or not?" Mira seems to be getting agitated.

Either the receptionist is trying to make a fool out of them or it's her genuine query. Priya is awestruck at the place itself and she is looking at the pretty receptionist who has put on so much of makeup, is in all black attire. It's Priya's first time that she has come to a "salon". She usually prefers to go to a clean ladies' parlour or with her mom's convenience, one is called at home. She had heard weird things happen at the salons. Since then, she was a bit scared to enter them. Thinking about that makes her get a bit uncomfortable.

The receptionist takes them to their respective rooms and tells them to get comfortable. Priya feels a bit scared and says, "Can I just get my pedicure done, please? I don't want anything."

Mira comes to her to console, "You ok, P. What happened? You don't want to get done anything, it's ok. I'll come some other day. I just wanted us to get pampered. It's my treat, babe. I only thought we would get our mani-pedi and hair spa or hair colouring done. If you don't want that, we can skip."

Priya realises she was having a panic attack. Why...she didn't understand. But after Mira consoles her, she feels a bit calm. The spot boy brings a glass of water for her. At first, she refuses and then when Mira gives her the glass, she gulps it down. She suddenly remembers that before reaching here they discussed about all this. But she wanted to pay on her own for herself. She takes Mira aside and tells her, "I am sorry again, M...I don't know what came over me. I just felt paralysed for a moment there. Can I just request you to be with me? Can we just start with mani or Pedi? And frankly, I just thought of getting the Pedi done, as I love my feet. Also, I would rather pay for me. I wouldn't want the money coming between us. I am not sure why I am so sensitive these days!"

"Alright. Whatever you feel comfortable in. It's probably that time of the month for you. Maybe this is why you're feeling a bit sensitive. Relax. I am with you, next to you. Let's just enjoy, okay?" Mira sounds brightly concerned.

And they both sit in an open room, where there are young ladies and men attending to their customers. There are a few ladies, maybe in their 40s who are getting their spa treatment along with their manicures simultaneously. They are probably enjoying every bit of it. They are both given a very comfortable massage chair which has a massage mechanism with a remote control. They savour the moment. "Are you okay, P?" Asks Mira softly.

"Thanks babe. Is this heaven? I have never felt so calm and at peace. This is fun. The water feels so nice."

"Doesn't it? I love getting my pedicure done mostly from here along with my hair. They do a brilliant job. So, you let me know when do you want to order, because since we are just getting this done, we should order or you want to get out of here and go to some café?" Inquires Mira.

Priya expresses, "How about we just go to my place, watch a movie with popcorn or just talk with coffee or chai?"

"Sounds really good, P! Let's just enjoy now." Utters Mira.

And they both close their eyes to relish the moment....

* * * * *

CHAPTER 7

Unwanted Guests

"Unwanted guests are like cursed spells-they arrive unbidden, linger too long, and only vanish when the magic word is finally spoken: Goodbye."

On their way back from the salon, they head into a café not very far from the salon, they each buy a nice cup of coffee, a pizza slice and a chicken club sandwich to go. They seem to be big enough for two. While they wait, Priya steps out and sees a shop which has all kinds of namkeens and chips and juices and drinks. She buys two packets of popcorns and some dairy milk chocolates for her family and Mira. As she is walking back to the café, her phone buzzes. It's a message from Saket. "Are u guyz ok? Hope u're not fightin?"

Priya texts back, "All good. 😊"

Mira is stepping out when Priya reaches. "That was fast. I was barely gone for 5 minutes! They seem really fast!" Reacts Priya.

"Touche!" responds Mira. "Let's head to your place, now."

"I was about to say that." Squeaks Priya. And yet again, her phone buzzes. This time it's a call from her mom. "Priya, how long for you to reach home?"

"Ma, we are on our way back. It'll take us another 5 minutes to reach. Is there anything you require?" Priya sounds obedient.

"No beta. Just come. Wanted to know how long you would take." Her mom replies. And the call is disconnected.

As soon as they reach home, Priya sees a sedan car parked outside the house. She wonders who would have come at this hour. They go in and hear a shrill and a manly voice. She understands it's the devil sisters of her grandmom, who out of the blue have come to pay a visit. Or rather one can say to see how everyone is doing. Priya doesn't pay heed to them and quietly walks past those two. She remembers the last time she met them; how much they had managed to insult her parents in front of her. She could not bear to see it happen again. She looks at her mom and asks her, "Since when are they here?"

She answers, "They came half an hour ago. And looks like they might stay till evening tea. So, I would request that you stay in your room. I have called your father to tackle them as I am in no mood to handle these two by myself. I believe they planned to come on a Saturday, knowing that you have an off and your father has to go. They came as soon as he left. And I am well aware what they are here for." Mom seems a bit agitated. But then probably talking to Priya makes her calm and she understands that she doesn't need to worry. Priya lets her know that she is around and suggests to her mom, "I know I shouldn't be saying this but I think we should remain in the kitchen, you and I, so they know you're busy. I am not sure if they saw me, even if they did, I guess I will be more disrespectful if I go there to greet them, so I'd rather stay here with you, till Papa comes."

Her mom says, "Better said than done, sweetie. And you're right, we cannot be more disrespectful than behaving like we are. You have Mira with you, you go tend to her. She must be waiting. What will you both eat?" She ends up asking this.

"Ma, you seriously don't have to worry about us. For now, we have our pizzas and a sandwich with us. We can manage." Priya kind of whispers.

Mira comes into the kitchen, "Dude, is everything ok? Why are you guys whispering? Who has come? Should I leave? I could come back later. Or maybe I could help." Mira says politely. She even asks her mom if they plan to hire a part-time help, to which her mom replies, "We aren't getting any. The ones who come, they are asking for a lot! Some say that they won't do this or that. Basically, it's a bit difficult. We do have a cleaning lady. But we haven't found someone who could help out in the kitchen as such. So that's that!"

Mira hears her mother, and looks at Priya and tells her, "P, I am going to let my mom know to arrange one for you. In fact, I will let her know right away!" she runs to the room to grab her phone and starts to text her mother. While she is texting, Priya's father comes home. He keeps his bag, comes into the kitchen, washes his hands, talks to mom, and goes to greet the ladies.

They both go and sit with them. Priya and Mira take over the kitchen. Priya makes coffee and Mira takes out the snacks from the pantry. While Mira is setting up the tray, her phone buzzes and she immediately takes it and reads, “Have arranged for a cook. He will come and talk to your mom in an hour. You were lucky enough to text now. He called to say he needed a place to stay and get work.”

Mira quickly texts back, “Thanks, ma. Does he have a family that he needs a place to stay?” And she asks Priya, “Dude, a cook has been arranged but tell me something, do you have a servant quarter or something? I believe you were lucky enough as my mom says that he just asked her for a job!”

“I believe we do! As a matter of fact, the garage area has a room with a kitchenette and a bathroom, so he could use that.” Replies Priya.

Mira then adds, “Mom says he has a kid and a wife. They left their village to work.”

Priya pauses for a moment and says, “Dude, what did you tell your mom?”

“I simply asked her and she said he is on his way; he must have taken some money from her for commuting. She says he’ll be here soon.” Mira responds casually.

Priya makes the coffee, sets them on the tray and takes it where everyone is sitting. She hears one of them say, “This is the one who bluntly said no to marriage.

This generation doesn't understand that getting married doesn't mean the end of life, it just means that life becomes better. She is not doing anything that she wants to escape the concept of getting married. She is not supposed to be staying now with her parents. She belongs to another house!" Priya, at first just ignores them, then she signals her mother to come out for a moment. Her mother does and they both tell her all about the servant. She seems relieved. She thanks Mira and lets her know that she would personally would like to thank her mother. Then Priya goes back to the living room and sits next to them. And starts to talk with her father sitting opposite her. "Namaste aunties, if you have come here to loathe and gather the gossip about us, please go ahead, I will not stop you, but if you have come here to talk about my marriage, then listen very carefully- I am the daughter of this house and will always remain one. Marriage will certainly start a new life, but at a great cost. When there are people like you around, life cannot be smooth. It is and will always remain a girl's choice to get married. People like you cannot decide for their time to get married. Now, lastly, I would humbly request you both to finish your lovely coffee, made by me and leave us be so that we can get on with our routine life, thank you very much!"

Papa gives Priya a proud look. And as her mom enters, she is stunned with their looks and silence. "What just happened?" she murmurs to papa.

Papa lifts his hand in a calming gesture, trying to reassure her that everything is under control. Mom becomes a little tense but she doesn't say a word. The ladies finish their coffee, take a few snacks. As they keep picking a biscuit or a chip, they smile at mom. Priya whispers in her father's ears, "They seem pretty sly! They have some nerve to pass a smirk at mom!" But she doesn't really respond.

Finally, one of them get up and say, "I think we'll take your leave, then. We'll see you around! You all should come over sometime."

"I believe the words you're looking for are, let's not meet at all! I would let my grandma know." Priya sounds polite yet she's blunt. They all bid them a goodbye. As they are entering back into the house, they hear an auto stop at their gate. They turn around to see who it is this time, Mira comes running out, holding her phone in her ear, screaming, "P, THEY'RE HERE!! I BELIEVE THIS IS A GOOD DAY!"

Priya holds her hand and asks, who she's talking to. She replies, "It's my mom. She was just calling up to let me know that your help is here. And she is telling me to come home for now. I might see you tonight. I am not sure."

"Why do you have to go? You were supposed to stay! Please, don't go yet. Now we would have so much fun. We had plans to watch a movie! Remember, we got popcorns and sandwiches and a pizza...."

"Okay, how about I meet you in the evening? Till then you meet the new comers, relax and tell your mom to relax as well. Although I know it's going to be hard initially. But I know you can handle everything! So, I will take your leave, and I'll see you when I can." Mira seems in a rush now.

"Ohh Mira!! I forgot to mention.... Sameer texted. He said he wanted to meet for coffee...." Priya is not able to complete her sentence and Mira cuts through.

"Really!!! That is fantabulous babe!!! When did this happen? What did you reply to him?"

"Aren't you getting late, now? Priya teases Mira.

"Well, yeah. But you had better promise me that you will tell me all about it when I get back!" Mira sounds enthusiastic. "Have you replied to him yet, by the way?" she asks excitedly.

"Not yet. I am still thinking and can't figure it out what to say, despite getting goosebumps by just thinking about it! And at the same time, I am having butterflies in my stomach! What am I supposed to say, I am completely blank at this point of time!" Priya confesses, a smile spreading across her face. "You just come back and then we'll talk." Priya is blushing. "See ya!" she says.

As she enters back into the house, she hears her parents talk about the episode. She chooses to ignore them and goes into the kitchen to drink a glass of water. She goes back into her room, cleans up the mess. And plops down on her cozy bed. She then takes out her diary and begins to write her feelings.

Dear Diary,

Today has been a weird day! Why is it that women have to be so nasty and bitchy? Does marriage make them like that? I sometimes wonder if my boldness would make me so much bitchier like them! I feel that happiness, love and respect are mostly that matters in a marriage. I also haven't really understood why middle-aged women want to get the young girls married! Why can't girls simply be left to live the lives they envision for themselves? I am feeling a sudden rage has gotten over me! It's like the outside world is not agreeing with me anymore! I honestly should get rid of this rage. I wonder how! I remember my father telling me once that I should listen to some devotional songs. It helps one become calm. I haven't really done that but I sure do believe in God. There are multiple ways to vent out:

1. *I could go out for a brisk walk with music in my ears.*
2. *I could paint or draw.*
3. *I could simply listen to my favourite songs.*
4. *I could write, which I do, often, not every day.*
5. *I could watch a movie.*
6. *I could attend a cooking class.*
7. *I could cook or bake something with Mira.*

So, my dear diary, I guess, we'll be meeting almost every day. And sometimes I'll be releasing my tensions on to you! ;-) If I miss out, I am sure I would catch up. But don't be disheartened if your pages fill up; each one holds a piece of my story.

Furthermore, I have a confession. I have been having these headaches often. I am not sure what to make of them. Haven't really told anyone, and I also know it's not much to mull over. But I am not sure who I should share this with. I sure hope no one grabs you unless I allow them to. I think I should let my parents know before it gets any worse. I hear you, diary! Till then, keep my stories a secret.

Love, Priya.

* * * * *

CHAPTER 8

Dear Diary!

"A diary doesn't judge, it only listens-my truest confidant."

As Priya sets down her diary; it being a weekend, when there's no class or activity, she has forgotten all about the exams that would be starting form Monday, she glances around her room, taking in the chaos that surrounds her. She finds a few bits of dust bunnies at the corners of her room. She decides to tackle some of the disorder. She remembers that she hadn't placed her music system properly. So, she goes to the open space where her mother has placed the brooms and a few other cleaning supplies; she picks up the broom and the dust collector, goes back into her room and starts to clean up the mess. As she starts with the cleaning, she shifts the tables and chairs, causing an inevitable clatter, and her mother gets drawn to all this commotion. When she sees her daughter being so engrossed in the cleaning, she feels so touched that she calls for the new house maid to help. The lady whose name is 'Laxmi', knocks on Priya's door. Priya gets impressed and lets her in. "Didi, aap kyun kar rahe ho, mujhe do, main saaf kar deti hoon. Aap mujhe hi bula lete." ("Sister, why are cleaning, give me I will do it for you. You should have called me.")

"Arre, kuch nahin hota. Main apna kamra khud hi saaf kar leti hoon. Aap pehle nahin thi, tab to karti hi thi!" Priya says cheerfully. (Arre, it doesn't matter. I prefer to clean my room myself. I was still keeping it clean before you.)

They both help each other and clean up the entire room. Soon after they are done, Priya thanks Laxmi. She leaves her room saying, "Didi, aapko jab bhi aapka kamra saaf karana ho, aap mujhe bula lena, main aapki madad kar doongi safai karvane mein. Kyunki aap bahut achhi ho."

(Sister, whenever you need my help, I will always come to help you. Because you are very nice.)

Priya returns a smile to her and says, "Okay, thank you!" And she closes her door.

As she is about to jump on to her bed, she sees a box peeking at her. She sits down and takes out the box, opens it and finds her old diaries. She remembers she started writing a diary when she was in class 9th. She recollects the time when she was a school head girl and how she managed to win the badminton tournament, by just a point. And she also commemorates to when she had mumps and had an in-grown toe-nail, where she had to wear slippers to school, which seemed odd to her then, and still does. When she had mumps, it was a difficult time for her as she was in so much pain, that couldn't eat her favourite comfort food. All she could eat was soup. She hated dal-water. She felt sick even thinking about it. Coming back to reality, she picks her top most diary, which according to her was almost filled, keeps it on her bed. Then she turns the curtains, makes the room dark, turns on her bed side lamp, takes her pillows and gets comfortable; finally, she takes her diary and begins to read. As she flips through the pages, she scans the pages and the words she had written months ago-her hopes, her fears and her secrets spilling over in a cursive-messy handwriting. A faint smile tugs at her lips as she rereads a poem she wrote for her mother and herself.

"Dear Diary,

I am feeling enthusiastic today. I am full of emotions and love for my mom. And I am super glad that I am a girl/woman! So, I have thought of this:

I, am a woman
Full of life, full of love.
Even full of emotions.
I, am a woman,
With elegance, beauty and passion.
I give, I even take.
I, am a woman.
Even called an aunt, a mom, a granny.
Some even make me a nanny.
I work, I play. I bake and make people smile,

Even wry.
I slog, I cry.
I am ordered, but I try.
I, am a woman
I love unconditionally.
I bear pains, I get wrinkles and pimples easily.
I, am a girl, when I am young,
I am a daughter doted on.
I am forced to get married-
And be a woman!
I, am a woman.
I can be aggressive,
Even selfish.
But I am willing to rely, love and respect.
For who I am.
I, am a woman!"
'Loads of love,
Priya'.

Priya feels overwhelmed, she gently closes her diary. A bittersweet sigh escapes her lips. The emotions she poured into the poem-resurface like a distant echo. She leans back against the pillows, staring at the ceiling, closes her eyes and reminisces to few other poems that she wrote, when she felt she was loaded with all kinds of emotions. She even becomes aware that since then she hasn't really written any more poems. Probably because she grew out of that particular phase or maybe she didn't contemplate enough. That said, she opens her diary again to the time when she remembers she was a bit tensed and depressed when her maternal grandmother fell ill. Although she was not too close to her, but she still liked her. She went through a time where she felt helpless. She couldn't understand how she could be more supportive to her mother. So, she wrote:

Dear diary,

I am not sure how I should explain this today. I wish I were more understanding and more supporting, somehow. I wish someone could come and talk and I could tell them how I am feeling right now!

So much pain,

So many cries,

Such less time,

Still no reply!

There's hope, there's faith.

Even the wild flowers have faded.

So much chaos,

So much panic.

Give me the strength,

To hold it all.

Bring in the happiness,
Bring in the smile.
Let it come, let it come,
Say all souls.
It rains, it pours,
He says there's more.
We are brave, we will save,
All the more.
So let it pour.
We will sing, we will dance,
We will be merry through it all!

I have tears in my eyes. I wish I could just……

Priya.

She closes the diary, lays down, and closes her eyes. In no time, she falls asleep, with her diary tucked under her arm. Probably her crying makes her doze off or maybe her mental exhaustion, which she only knew.

Its's nearly 3 pm. There's a knock on her door. She doesn't wake up. Then there's banging on her door. BANG!! BANG!! BANG!! Startled by the sudden noise, she jolts awake. Her heart is pounding and she feels disoriented. "Who is it?" She gets up, walks towards her door and opens it. It's her brother. "You need to come and have your lunch, madam. Mom is furious. She's been calling you for the past half an hour. But you never listen! She even called you. Where the heck is your phone? You better start answering your phone else it will be taken away; do you even know that?!"

"Vedu, you really need to shut up! How much can you talk?! I never got any calls from anyone. Why do like troubling me so much!" Priya sounds mildly frustrated.

"Because I am your brother. And this is what brothers do! They love to trouble their sisters and get them into trouble!" Says Vedant, sounding pleased with himself. "Let's go and have your lunch. Mom is waiting. She says we are already late in having our lunch, she is feeling a bit tired so she wants to rest for a while. Then in the evening they have to go out for dinner to their friends' home." He sounds soft and gentle this time.

"You go ahead, I'll just come in 2 minutes."

"Don't doze off again. This time mom would actually be furious." Teases Vedant.

"Yeah! You go, sit, I am coming." Priya quickly rushes to the bed, gathers her diaries, shoves them back into the box and hides it under her bed once more.

She retains that Mira was supposed to come. Before leaving the room, she grabs her phone, decides to text her. "Whr the heck r u? u ver suppsd 2 cm bak?! M w8ing. Call me or txt me, pls"

And she goes to the dining room, her mom and Vedu have already started. She sits on her chair, serves on her plate, and quietly starts to eat slowly. She looks at her mother, who is engrossed in her eating with a book. Priya loves this about her mother. But sometimes it becomes too much for her to handle as she forgets about everything else while reading! Which only means, that she is enjoying her book. Anyways, Priya recalls that she has some major work to do, read a few stories about her past, she quickly finishes off her food and puts back her plate in the kitchen and lets her mom know that she enjoyed the food and now she wants to go back to sleep. "Why are you in a hurry to sleep, beta? Are you feeling sick?' her mom calls out, sounding concerned.

Priya comes back to reply, "I am absolutely fine, ma. Just have some work to do- just some college stuff. Need some time to think about it and then start working on it. So, all good." Priya smiles and goes back.

Vedant raises a suspicious eyebrow, but the cheeky grin makes him look mischievous. Mom immediately, sternly lets him know, "Vedu, don't even think about it! You are not going to ruin her day off. I seriously don't want any kind of commotion or racket while I rest! I hope I am loud and clear about this! She is not troubling you in any way, why should you?! She probably has a lot going on in her mind and her life. So, just let her be."

Vedu's mischievous grin dims, leaving a hint of it behind. He finishes his lunch, asks to be relieved, puts back his plate in the kitchen sink, and goes to his sister's room, knocks and then goes in. "Didi, are you feeling alright? You had too little and got up to come to your room. Is there anything that's troubling you?"

"I am ok, bro! What made you think I am not ok? I was just going through my stuff as I cleaned my room. There was so much of mess so I thought of cleaning it, since I had the time. What's with you? Are you ok?" Priya asks calmly. She had an inkling that he would come to trouble her, so she was careful enough to not open any diaries. Instead, she took out some college papers pretended to look at them as if she was adjusting them.

"All good. Just thought to come and trouble you. ;-) Just kidding. You carry on. I'll leave you to it, then. I'll be in my room. I have homework to do." Vedant sounds like he is expecting to be stopped, but there is no such response from Priya. Rather she says, "Ok, just close the door behind when you leave."

Finally, when he leaves, she runs to lock her door. She swiftly retrieves her box, carefully pulls out her box of diaries, and begins arranging them meticulously. She checks the dates, placing the oldest diary at the bottom and stacking the others in chronological order. Then she takes her current diary from the bedside drawer and places it neatly beside her.

She opens her previous diary and goes through it. Turns to the page that she last read. She flips the pages again and comes to the story when she was driving her grandmother's car. She reads:

Dear diary,

Today as I went to visit my grandmother, she had some work that she had to do. So, she went off with one of her sisters in their car. And she left her own at home. Grandpa was busy watching the news. I asked him if I could borrow the car and go out to buy something. Usually when he is with grandma, he prefers to be as strict as her, but today he was absolutely cool and said yes! I was excited and plus I was glad that I was getting a chance to practice my driving. So, I took the keys, started the engine and took off. I did my work. It took me good half an hour as first I had some work at the bank, and then I had to go buy some books. As I was returning, I saw a little furry pup hovering in the middle of the road. It looked lost and was probably searching for its mom. This is an Indian roads problem. A cow and a dog can appear at any time, from anywhere. So many of these animals are harmed and killed in accidents every single day. They are tortured by hooligans and dumb people. Their life is not at all easy, and we cry for our lives. So, as I was saying, I was driving back, it was the main road, and a cute puppy seemed lost. I stopped my car at that very moment, I was kinda stopping the traffic behind me, but I did not care, I stepped out of the car, picked up that pup and took it on to the side of the road. For a moment I thought of taking it with me. But then I remembered, it would be a lot hard work to handle a puppy. And I was not ready for it just now. So, I simply, took it away from the main road. Luckily a man came running saying that he was taking care of these puppies.

This one wandered off. He thanked me, though. It was at first unusual for me, but then I saw his tattered clothes. I saw a cart with little packets of sweet tamarinds and 'aam papad'. It looked as if nobody was buying from this poor guy. So, I decided to give him some money. I wondered how he was managing feeding those puppies if he said he was taking care of them. Better still, I went ahead and gave him some more money and told him that he was doing a good job taking care of the animals. Suddenly, it struck me that I could tell him to join an Animal Rescue Center. That way he could get paid, somehow. I don't know why, but I did feel the urge to help this guy. So, I gave him my number, by writing it on the piece of paper. Surprisingly, he knew how to read! this gave me a reason to respect the guy. It turned out, when asked his name, he replied, "Rakesh...I study till class 10, then my phather beat me coz I asked for extra class. And he had no money, only to drink. So, I left house and come to Dilli." That sounded pretty awesome, na, Diary?! I was amazed. So, I decided that I had to help this guy. I told him to come and meet me at my grandmother's house. I wrote the address and told him I would help him get a proper job and he should bring his cart and his puppies along. He agreed immediately. I felt proud at that moment. I sat back in my car and drove back. This incident took me about 45 minutes. When I reached home, my grandmother was pacing around and my grandfather was sitting on his favourite chair, watching her. I went ahead and asked about her worry. She replied, "Where did you go? We were getting worried. I had told your Babaji to not let you go out. He doesn't listen and nor do you. What was the need to go just now?! What was so important that you had to go from here? You could have gone from your parent's place!" I was really upset and angry, diary! So, I just told her, I had to buy some college books that were now available. And I only happened to save a little puppy from an accident...is all. This is what took me time. You don't have to yell so much. I had my phone with me. You could have simply called and asked. And plus, you are aware of the traffic here! Now, let's not talk anymore. When you calm down, then we'll talk. Till then, let's stay away from each other's way."

I said this and went ahead to Babaji and told him the rest of the incident. He felt really happy and gave a pat on my back. He promised to gift me a nice music system. I refused at first, but then he insisted and I couldn't say no. he felt relieved that I managed to find a man for him who he would keep or maybe help. I earned this good day and it felt so good. It felt as if I had achieved something! Till next time.

Loads of love,

Priya.

After reading this entry, Priya realised she had completely forgotten about the incident. And since that time, her grandmother had started to plan to get rid of her by getting her married. Only because she gave it back to her. And she didn't feel guilty at all. She perceived that she was savouring that moment of reading about herself without any distractions or interference. She only felt as if somehow, she could just visualise herself in those moments or look at the picture of them. Also, that man Rakesh still works for them as their driver. He does a double duty for them and works as a guard as well, and feels obliged to my grandfather. He sure is a hard worker.

She looks at the time and notices it was nearly 5 pm, and there was still no news from Mira. So, she sets her diary aside, but then it hits her-just moments ago, she was fully immersed in the moment, and now, she finds herself longing for Mira's presence, yet unable to do what she wishes to do! She picks up her phone, and sees that she has a few missed calls from Mira and a text. She opens the message and it reads, 'Stuk wid mom. Wl call u whn m free. Sorry 2 hv missd ur msg'

She doesn't understand if she should take a sigh of relief that she is getting a chance to be by herself or should she get angry that they were to be together today and discuss about Sameer. She figured that if Mira has said that she would call back, she became comfortable.

Ultimately, she feels content and gets back to her reading. She flips a few pages together and skips some in between, she comes to the page where she was once really upset when she was slapped by her grandmother, only for ruining her white suits.

Dear Diary,

Today was the worst day ever! I hope that this is the one and only day that I have been slapped by my grandmother. The day started as any other normal day. It was a holiday. My grandmother was visiting us as she just wanted to. The maid at our place was on leave. Unfortunately, my mom had to take care of the chores. Luckily, we had a washing machine and I knew how to operate it. These days, my mom goes for a workshop to learn to bake cookies and cakes. So, she was getting late as it was a morning class, being a Saturday. She went with papa. I woke up a bit late, went to the kitchen to make myself a cup of tea. I saw that my grandmother was trying to fiddle with the machine. I went to her and asked her what she was up to. I saw that she was trying to start the machine. I bent down to see that there weren't any clothes in there. I simply asked her why she was toying with the washing machine. She just denied that she was playing with it. She was only trying to turn it on. So, I asked her, "when there are no clothes, why are you trying to turn it on. You bring your clothes; I'll turn it on for you." She quickly agreed and brought her clothes. I put them inside. I put in some detergent and switched it on. Then I went to make myself a cup of tea. My grandmom came into the kitchen and asked me if she could make me as she was also going to have some. I told her if she could tolerate a strong ginger tea, she was most welcome to help. While she was making the tea, I thought I could go and brush my teeth. As I went it, Vedant came out holding a red shirt in his hand. He asked me if the machine is turned on, he wanted to put his clothes also for wash. I told him he could wait. Probably he didn't hear me or what, he put his shirt in. I came out after brushing my teeth, she was standing near the machine with her hands on her forehead. She seemed really upset. I went and asked her why was she upset. She got up and gave me a slap. It came pretty hard on my cheek that I felt numb and thought I lost my hearing. Next thing I remember, I had tears flowing down my cheeks. I couldn't stop crying. Luckily, my parents returned, as they entered and saw me crying, they asked what had happened. She told them that I had put a coloured cloth with white clothes. I didn't know that at first. My father came to me and asked me, "What happened, Priya?" I looked at him and told him that I was not aware of the incident. And I never put the coloured shirt in there. He looked up and glanced at Vedant's door. By then I had started having a headache. My mom just stood there talking to her, telling her she had no right hitting me! Papa went to Vedant's room and asked him if he had put in the coloured shirt in the running washing machine. He said he did, but he wasn't aware that there were no coloured clothes, he just put it in there. Papa looked really upset and went to his mother and told her loudly, "You will not touch her again. You come and talk to me if you have a problem with her. You are never ever going to talk to her. I will not tolerate you hitting her for no reason! Please stay away from her. Now, I would request you to kindly go back to your place."

At that point, I felt relieved but it hurt a lot. I didn't feel like talking to anyone, so I came into my room and lay back down. I didn't even have my breakfast. I guess I dozed off again.

Till next time!

Priya.

Priya recalls that the next day she woke up with a sharp pain on her left side where she got slapped. When her father checked her, it had started to swell up a little, so he took her to a doctor and it turned out to be 'mumps'. Gosh! That was some experience! For an entire week and a half, she survived on soup. She couldn't eat or chew anything! She then flipped back some pages and read through the part where she had named her diary as 'Betty'. At that time Priya was going through an odd phase. She browsed her mother's library and came across her collection of Archie comics. She relished all the ones she read. It gave her immense pleasure in reading those comics. She loved the character of betty. She thought of becoming a bit like her so she kind of started moulding herself a bit by learning to do everything by herself, cleaning up her room, decorating her room like Betty's.

Suddenly, there's a knock on the door. "Priya bete! Is everything ok? Why have you locked the door?" It's her father. He has returned from his work. She quickly unlocks her door and lets him in. "Are you feeling alright? Mom told me you didn't eat your food properly. I thought to come and check up on you!" He sits on the chair and makes her sit in front of him. He touches her forehead, but then shakes his head that there's no fever. Priya says, "Papa, I am fine. I just wanted some time for myself without any disturbance, that's all." He nods his head and says, "Okay."

Her father always made sure that whenever he returned from his work, he used to make sure to say 'hello' to both of them in their respective rooms, if they weren't around to greet him in the living room.

Just before he leaves, all he says is, "Bete, try not to lock your door and just eat your food properly. I wouldn't want you falling ill."

"Yes, papa! Don't worry." Priya smiles at him.

"Care for a pizza or something? My treat!" Asks papa lovingly.

"If you insist! That I could never say no to!" Replies Priya as lovingly.

Whilst talking to her father, Priya receives a message from Mira, "On my way 2 u, finally!"

Priya gets excited and asks her father, "Papa, are you seriously getting pizzas?"

"Yes baby! You want to come along?" He asks.

"Not really. Can I just ask for a large one, whichever you're getting?" She sounds coyish. Although at that moment she also feels guilty for saying no to going with him. For a moment, she falls back into the time when she used to go with her father for a round to buy 'gol-gappas' and 'jalebis' on his scooter when she was little. She also remembered that his scooter was grey-black with two separate seats.

She learnt to sit like a girl as her father taught her, when she was growing. And immediately, she yells, "Papa, I want to come!" She quickly wears her slippers, takes her phone and texts Mira, "Going 2 get pizza wid papa. Will c u whn I get bak."

Pretending to be a carefree little girl brimming with excitement to ride with her father, she sets aside all her worries and savours the moment. She settles onto the backseat, wraps her arms tightly around her father, the wind rushing through her hair.

When they come back after getting the pizza, Mira is waiting in Priya's room, going through her cassettes; probably planning on listening to some good music. Maybe she is in a good mood or maybe she was glad to be with Priya or may be both! "And you're back, finally! What happened? You took like.... forever! Where did you go with your mother? What was so important? Never mind! Pizza is finally here! And it was so much fun going on papa's scooter! I was reliving my childhood...It felt great! I am pretty happy right now.... I don't know why.... but I feel good!"

"Good to know, P! I believe after quite a while you have become happy. I think last I saw you happy was the day we went to the mall; you were something else then! We had loads of fun, remember?!"

"Yeah! At present I just feel that all my worries have sort of disappeared. I am glad to have a father like him, you as my friend, Vedant as my brother, my mom, who will be starting as a Principal from July in The Gurukul School. And we are going to have our exams from day after, that is Monday, which we aren't completely prepared for.... AAAAAAAAhhhhhhhhhh!!! Mira, we will have to pull an all-nighter to perform in the exam! Are you even prepared a little? I am not at all prepared! Shit!! What's going to happen now!"

Mira gets up, holds Priya's hands, tell her to calm down. "You need to breathe! Relax...we have time! This isn't the end of time that you're panicking so much! Let's sit and like you just said, we can pull an all-nighter, only if required. Our first is English which we can pull through. And there's a break between, so we will be able to make it. Our exams would go on for 15 days. That means we have enough time to study for them...ok?!"

"Are you asking or telling?" Priya asks still seeming tensed.

"I am calming myself too!" Replies Mira, who is also sounding like she is about to go into a panic mode.

Instead of chatting much, they choose to study together, pulling an all-nighter in the process. They help each other clear doubts, work through practice papers, and quietly solve questions side by side. To test their knowledge, they quiz each other, identifying gaps and tackling the answers they don't yet know.

By 5 a.m., they are utterly exhausted, having powered through the night fuelled only by water and sheer determination to complete their studies. A sense of relief washes over them as they decide to catch up on four hours of sleep, setting their alarms before settling down. Priya curls up on the floor mattress while Mira takes the bed, surrounded by scattered books. The air-conditioner hums softly, but the fan remains off, and a slight chill fills the room. Priya's father peeks in to check on them, smiles at the sight of their sleepy state, and quietly shakes his head. He steps out briefly, returning with a blanket to cover them both, noticing they might be feeling cold. He understands that they stayed up all night, so he doesn't make a single sound and walks out, gently pulling the door to close. He lets the family know about the girl's situation and comes to a conclusion that this would be a scenario for the next 13 days. Priya and Mira had taken a pact to study and live together till the exams were over. This way they thought was helpful in every way for the both of them.

* * * * *

CHAPTER 9

Sameer's Surprise!

"A true surprise is not just unexpected; it's unforgettable!"

A night before their last exam, Priya sits with Mira after dinner and asks her, "Don't you wanna know about the text conversation Sameer and me had?"

"Ohhh yeah! I completely forgot about that! Tell me, tell me everything!" Mira sounds excited.

"Well, he just wanted to meet for coffee! I haven't exactly replied to him." Priya says shyly.

"Excuse me! May I ask why you haven't replied to him, till yet?" Mira sounds a bit agitated now.

"Well, the day he texted, you and I had a miscommunication cum misunderstanding, remember? It's been a while and then we've been having our exams...so, haven't really had a chance to text him back. He said he was aware that I have a liking towards him. Is that to do with you? Because you are the only one, I know who could communicate with him and let him know something like this!"

Mira looks down, trying to pretend to not know what Priya was talking about. Priya catches her neck playfully, to find out the truth. "Well, I might have uttered something like this to him, by mistake. It was unintentional, but with a good heart. It did you good, na!" Mira tries to sound convincing.

"Don't do that, M. I honestly don't like that people are forced to like me. If we are to be together, we will be. You or I cannot make someone love or be loved. I barely know him, but I find him to be good-looking, he's smart and seems caring. But what if I am not up to his liking? We should know each other enough to like or love each other." Priya becomes gloomy.

"Well, this is your opportunity, P. I will **promise** you this that from here on, I will not play a cupid. I will let you both be and you both can play it out the way you feel is right. But I have only opened a door for you. Step in and see what it has in store for you." Mira becomes optimistic.

"Okay. I will take your word for it. And I will forgive you for letting him know about my feelings. I will text him tomorrow after the exam...."

Mira cuts her short, "No P, you will text him, now! I mean it. It's been too many days. Please text him that you will meet him for coffee, tomorrow."

Priya has to give in to Mira's persuasiveness. "Ok, I will text him, but can we finish with our studies first, please? We have an exam tomorrow, which is more important than Sameer or the text right now! By the way, is he aware about the exams?"

"Yes. He is also aware that they are ending tomorrow and then we start with our month and a half long break!" Mira says naughtily.

"I thought you said you weren't really much friendly with him! How is it that he gets to know everything now?!" Priya interrogates Mira.

Mira pretends to scold Priya and says, "Aren't we supposed to study? Don't we have an exam tomorrow? Let's study first and then we can discuss everything about him." Mira has a guilt look.

The next day, they are woken up by Priya's father. Their alarm probably doesn't go off. They hustle around, yelling, "Today's our last exam. We shouldn't miss it." They quickly get ready and finish their breakfast faster than ever and rush out. Priya is constantly thinking, *what if they don't let us in because of being late. What if they don't allow us to finish the paper and throw us out for being late.* All these thoughts come splashing in her mind, so she remains quiet throughout the car ride from home to college. Mira just drives, she also doesn't speak a word, probably same thoughts crossing her mind as well. They park the car, rush to their class room and sit in their respective places, they hear the bell ring, "Just in time!" Priya says with a sigh of relief. "I was really scared."

Mira too claims, "At some point, I was scared too. But glad we made it just in time."

As the bell rings, the invigilator steps into the classroom holding a stack of question papers. She carefully distributes them before summoning another professor to monitor from the back of the room, ensuring strict supervision. Priya and Mira exchange a quick smile when they glance at the paper, feeling confident in their preparation. With a thumbs-up, they quietly wish each other good luck and dive into the exam. Well-prepared, they navigate the questions with ease, finishing the 3-hour exam in just two and a half hours. However, the rules prevent them from leaving until the time is up, so they remain seated while others continue writing.

The bell rings again, they both step out, smiling and feeling happy. Then the next thing they do is check their phones. Priya receives a call from Sameer and she reminds herself to send him a message to meet for coffee, and a message from her father, and so does Mira. They both respond to their respective parents, calling back quickly. As they reach the parking lot, Priya hears a car horn blaring incessantly. She looks around and spots a sleek black Honda CBZ parked in front of them. The rider, dressed in blue denim and a linen shirt, has his helmet on, and the bike looks impressive from up-close. Mira, recognizing the bike, quietly steps into her car, while Priya remains standing, curious about the person who's blocked their car with the honking. The rider motions for her to sit behind him, but Priya gestures for him to move his bike. He doesn't budge, instead inching closer to her before taking off his helmet. Priya is left stunned when she sees his face—it's Sameer. She turns around in order to ask Mira, but finds her already sitting in her car, ready to leave them together. She signals her that she will call her in a while. She feels super shy, yet asks him, "How did you know we would be here and what time we will be coming out? This is a big surprise. I was about to text you."

"Well, I know you've been caught up with things and your exams. And now you know that I would know when your exams would be ending, so I thought of coming to take you myself. So, how about you hop onto my bike and let's go chill!" Sameer says smiling. Let's get to know each other and then we could decide and plan...what say?"

"Sounds good." Responds Priya as she doesn't know what else to say. As Priya hesitates for a moment, unsure of how to position herself, she recalls her father's lesson about proper posture when riding. The uncertainty makes her pause, but she decides to go with the moment. She swings her leg over the bike and sits with both legs on either side, feeling a sense of safety and balance. Her choice of light blue denim jeans and a comfy tee seems perfect for the occasion, adding to her sense of ease. To keep her hair from blowing wildly, she quickly ties it up in a neat bun, feeling a touch of relief that she managed to stay composed. She looks in the rear-view, and feels pretty. He waits for her to get comfortable and asks her if she is ready to move, she says, "Let's go!" And off they go.

As he rides, she gets a wave of nice fragrance, this fragrance takes her back to the time she first had this whiff, at that café, which made her swoon over him. She realises she has a soft smile on her face, just by thinking about it. She suddenly senses all kinds of feelings and thoughts crashing down on her. She feels like the luckiest person alive, imagining the envious looks of the other girls as she rides on the coolest bike, with the most handsome boy beside her. Her heart races as she pictures the attention they must be getting, all eyes on them as they cruise by. Her thoughts are broken when he asks, sliding his helmet's glass shield up, "What do you want to have?"

She asks back, "What do you mean?"

"Well," he begins, hesitating slightly, "Should we go to a nice restaurant, or are you in the mood for something more casual-like coffee with a burger or a sandwich? Or maybe you'd prefer a fast-food spot?"

She replies, "Let's go somewhere we can hear each other talk. Your choice."

He gives a thumbs-up and drives her to Vasant Vihar, where he surprises her with a visit to a charming open café simply named *The Café*. The ambience is breathtaking, a perfect blend of warmth and creativity. Its architectural design boasts a contemporary style, with vibrant, colourful walls accented by warm, inviting lighting. The flooring seamlessly complements the overall aesthetic, adding to the place's cohesive charm.

Behind the bar, a striking brick wall draws attention, while one side of the café features an artistic mural crafted from broken tiles, marbles, and mirrors. The tables are uniquely designed with coasters embedded in resin, giving each one a personal touch, and the wooden chairs are softened with cozy cushions. Certain corners are designed for relaxation, with low tables surrounded by floor cushions, creating snug, intimate spaces. Every detail of the café seems thoughtfully curated, leaving her thoroughly impressed.

As she enters the washroom, the quiet hum of the place soothes her nerves. The cool, refreshing splash of water on her face feels like a gentle reset, washing away the tension. The droplets feel calming against her skin. She grabs a tissue, gently dabbing her face dry, taking care to pat rather than rub. With a soft sigh, she releases her hair from the loose tie that had been holding it up. Carefully, she runs her fingers through it, combing it into place with practiced precision. Her hair falls in soft waves around her face, the neatness giving her a sense of control. She reaches for her lip balm and applies it to her slightly chapped lips, the smoothness of the balm providing instant comfort. Looking into the mirror, she meets her own gaze. She straightens her posture, tilting her head slightly, and whispers to herself, "I am pretty and I will be cool and calm." The words are a quiet affirmation, a reminder of the strength and poise she carries within.

She steps out of the washroom, the cool air of the hallway brushing against her skin. Her heart beats a little faster as she scans the room, searching for him. Her gaze lands on the familiar sight of a comfortable chair, nestled among plush cushions. It's the one she had noticed earlier, with its inviting, soft embrace.

There he is, sitting, relaxed yet composed. He doesn't seem to notice her at first, lost in his own thoughts, but the moment she approaches, his eyes lift. A soft smile tugs at the corners of his lips as he meets her gaze. It's as if the world has narrowed down to just the two of them, the room around them fading into the background.

She takes a step closer, feeling the flutter of anticipation in her chest. There's something about this moment, something familiar yet new, and she can't help but feel a sense of calm wash over her. She approaches him, her steps light and steady, drawn to the comfort of his presence. She sets herself across him. He leans forward and asks her, “What’ll you have, P? They have vada-pav, Maggi, pakoras, sandwiches, chai, cold coffee, chocolate smoothie, and...... I lost track after that. Too much to take in.”

“Why, haven’t you ordered anything for yourself yet?” She asks him politely.

“No. I was waiting for you. So, whatever you want to have. Or let’s call the person who will take our order, after he gives us the menu card.” He chuckles.

Priya raises her hand when she sees a guy to call him and mumbles, “Take the order?”

The boy comes and responses, “Yes ma’am. What can I get you?”

“Can we get a menu card, if you have or will you tell us today’s special?” She enquires. He responds, “I can get you the menu card as well as tell you today’s special menu.”

“Sounds good.” She looks at Sameer and he says, “Let’s get the menu, first.”

The boy quickly goes and gets the menu cards for both of them and waits for their response. Sameer chooses a cold coffee with a paneer sandwich. She prefers a chocolate smoothie with a Schezwan Maggi noodles. This menu seems outstanding and quite different. So, she asks him, “Where and how did you find this place?”

And he replies, "All the information about these new and trendy cafes comes in the city newspaper. Do you read any newspapers?"

"Not really, just sometimes, for general knowledge. I don't usually like to read the news, as it depresses me. I use it for different kinds of information though. But apart from that, not really." She says matter of factly. She realizes that an unusual sense of calmness has settled over her, with no trace of jitters. His presence has a way of making her feel at ease.

For a few minutes, both of them become quiet, Sameer speaks up in his husky tone, "So, Priya...let me say this... please don't mind, but look, I can actually sense that you're a bit nervous being here with me and, let me be absolutely honest, I am too! I am not completely sure what exactly to think, but in this moment, I am getting pretty comfortable with you."

Priya smiles and says in a soft tone, "Well, first of all, I am too becoming at ease with you. In fact, I was just thinking the same. It'll take me some time to completely open up in front of you. But to be honest myself, I am pretty nervous alright. So how about, we get to know about each other more and we can decide where this road takes us. I personally would leave this to the fate. Because I do like you, you're quite good looking, humble, chivalrous. So, this is me being genuinely straightforward."

"I like your integrity, Priya! I think you've said it." And while he is talking, their food comes. And there is a nice music playing in the background, and Priya says, "This looks and smells really good! But...." She pauses.

"Anything the matter, Priya? You, okay? Is it too spicy for you? Should I get it changed?" He asks concernedly.

"No...no. nothing...all good. Don't worry so much, Sameer. It's just, our family usually does this, so when we feel that the food will be left out, we get it packed, and take it home. I believe you'll find this funny and weird."

"Well, believe it or not, I don't find this funny or weird, I think it's nice to know this about you that you don't like to waste food. Point noted, ma'am." Sameer smiles softly.

"Oh my god, you are something, aren't you! Mam and all! You don't really have to be all formal with me. I will do this often if you insist, Monsieur!" Priya chuckles. "But jokes apart.

Let's enjoy the meal, and then after you will have to drop me back home. Hope you haven't forgotten that."

"Not at all, relax and enjoy. I am sure Mira must have handled the situation. I bet your parents aren't aware yet about Moi?!"

"That is correct. I will tell them once we are clear ourselves. My conscience says to keep mum about this as of now as I honestly don't want to jinx all this, the present!" Priya says and adds, "This moment is a 'present' for me, you see. About a month ago, I saw you, and wished for myself to date you or imagined it, and here we are! You gave a surprise, which will be unforgettable! And moments like these are cherished. So, thank you for making this day memorable for me, Sameer."

"You are most welcome, P. May I also call you P or is it too cliché for you? I am aware Mira calls you P, I wonder why she has this habit but she does." Sameer makes a friendly conversation. And when he sees the meals are done, he makes a gesture to call the guy to bring a check. As soon as the boy comes, he asks, "Sir, Mam, how was your meal? Was it to your satisfaction?"

Priya replies, "It was fantastic. We enjoyed thoroughly. Thank the chef for the amazing meal!"

The boy happily obliges and says, "Thank you so much, mam." And he takes the plates away and brings a black book kinda pouch with the bill. Priya intervenes and says, "Sameer, can we split the bill? It shouldn't be your responsibility to pay every time we go out. I might not be earning but, but I do get my pocket-money."

"That is very thoughtful of you, Priya. I will keep this in mind as well. But for today, it's my treat since I brought you here. We will discuss about this next time. So, sit back and relax when you're here with me." He pays and tips the boy. The boy cheerfully tells them to come again and opens the door for them. As they step out of the café, he tells her to wait, quickly runs away and comes back after 5 minutes, having a small bouquet and a chocolate box of 'Ferrero Rochers'.

"Here, these are for you. This is me acknowledging your company which I would love to have again!" He looks confident when he says so.

Priya's cheeks become red. She is speechless. All that comes out of her mouth is, "Thank you!" in a hushed tone.

She doesn't say another word, just has a big smile on her face. He asks her to sit on his bike, while he holds her flowers and chocolate box. Once she settles, sling hangs her bag sideways, then holds the flowers and he offers to keep the chocolate box in her bag. Priya hesitates for a moment before handing him her bag, her heart racing as she feels his presence so close. He carefully places the chocolate box inside, his fingers brushing against the fabric gently, as if it were as precious as her smile.

As he hands the bag back, their eyes meet briefly, a soft glimmer in his that makes her cheeks flush even deeper. Without saying a word, he adjusts the rearview mirror, ensuring she's seated comfortably, his every action deliberate yet thoughtful.

"Hold on tight", he says with a faint grim, his voice steady but warm.

She grips the sides of the seat nervously, unsure of how close to lean. Then as the bike hums softly beneath them, he tilts his head slightly back and asks, "Which way to your place?"

"Oh!" Priya fumbles, startled by his question, and points down the road, "It's straight for a while, then a left at the second signal. I'll guide you."

He nods, revving the engine gently. "Got it. let me know if I miss a turn."

The afternoon casts a glow on the bustling streets as they begin their ride. Priya clutches the seat, her heart pounding as the breeze sweeps her hair back. The scent of fresh flowers mingles with the crisp air, adding a sense of charm to the moment.

"You okay back there?" He asks after a while, glancing briefly over his shoulder.

"Yes." She replies quickly, her voice high pitched but sincere. "Just.... keep going straight for now."

At each turn, she carefully directs him, her voice growing steadier as the ride progresses. The city noise seems distant, the occasional chirping of birds and rustling trees framing the quiet bond forming between them.

When they finally approach her street, Priya points to a charming building at the end of the road. "That's my place, can you just stop a little away from the gate?" she requests him softly.

He slows down, pulling up where he's asked to stop. The sunlight catches on when he hands back the flowers to her.

"Thanks for letting me know the way," he says standing next to the bike now. "Not bad for a first-time navigator!"

"I know my routes", Priya laughs nervously, tucking a strand of hair behind her ear. "Thank you.... for everything", she says, clutching the flowers tightly.

He leans against the bike, the corners of his mouth lifting into a playful grin. "Next time, I'll let you pick the route."

The idea of a 'next time' sends her heart fluttering, but all she manages is a smile and a soft, "Drive safe."

The afternoon sunlight reflects off the rearview mirror as he waves lightly before riding off, leaving her standing where he left her, flowers in hand, her heart fluttering with a quiet joy that lingered like the soft warmth of the afternoon sun.

She starts to walk back to her home, a smile and blush not leaving her face. She opens her gate to walk in, and Vedant opens the door for her. "How was your exam, sis?"

Priya's thoughts vanish and she gets startled again. "My exam....it was good! What were you up to? Where are ma and papa?"

"Where did you get these flowers from.... I am really curious! Did you buy them or someone gave them to you? if you've bought them, then why? And if someone's given them to you, then who? I want to know else I will tell it to them and pester you for the rest of your life, Didi!" Vedu starts interrogating Priya.

"Okay, relax, I will tell you. But you have to promise me that you will not tell them a single thing. Else I will never talk to you nor help you with your projects!" Priya gives it back to him, sounding vindictive.

"Alright. I will be honest with you, because I love you and you're my silly brother.... So, I have a crush on this guy, who in return likes me back...."

"Okay, stop. I don't want to know any further details. You can talk about this all you want with Mira when she comes. By the way, all you could have mentioned is, you have a boyfriend now!! I would have confirmed that, silly girl!" Vedant pulls her hair and runs away. This time, she doesn't say anything to him. She just goes to his room, and unwraps the plastic wrap of the chocolate box and shares it with him. "Thanks", he goes and she smiles at him and goes to her room.

When she enters her room, she dumps her bag on the floor, her phone pings, it's Mira. She opens the message and reads, '*How was your day? I will see you in an hour. Keep all ur gossip ready.*'

Priya smiles at the message and suddenly remembers that she wants to know where her parents are. She runs to Vedu's room and, "Ma & Papa have gone to a friends' place, said something about someone being in the hospital, so they should come back soon. The food is in the kitchen if any of us are hungry." And he gets back to his playing on the computer.

Suddenly hearing the word- 'hungry', it strikes her that she had forgotten her Maggi at the café. Panic floods her mind as she imagines someone taking it or the boy simply throwing it away. She's desperate to call Mira, but then remembers that she had just messaged her, telling her she would be there in an hour. She wishes time could move faster, just for a moment, to ease her nerves.

She doesn't want to trouble Sameer over something so trivial, yet the thought of getting her Maggi back and possibly seeing him again seems like the only solution.

She begins pacing around her room, unable to settle, and in that moment, she pauses, wondering why she's acting this way. Then it hits her—she wants not only to retrieve her packed Maggi but also to meet Sameer once more.

She realises pacing around and getting panicky won't help in any way nor will Mira come so soon...so she decides she will only wait. She takes off her shoes and gets comfortable after climbing on her bed. She lays down and conks off. No sooner does the doorbell rings and she wakes up with a startle. "Hmmm.... what...!" she goes. And there's another time of the doorbell ringing, she runs out and Vedu also steps out, it's Mira and her parents, together.

"How come you guys have come together!! This is a surprise!" Priya reacts, still in a daze.

Mira touches her forehead, "Are you okay, P? Were you asleep? Seriously!! Without me!!!" She's literally shrieking, in a low tone.

"I am fine, you silly girl. Yes, I was asleep. Do you have a problem with that?! I am tired, so I dozed off for a bit." Priya is now beginning to sound as herself. Suddenly she remembers she has to go for the...." Mira, can you please come into my room, quickly, it's really urgent!"

"What's wrong?" she asks sounding concerned.

"Nothing to worry. It's just, I left the packed Maggi at the café that Sameer and I went to, it was a delicious one, and I forgot to bring it home for us to share. And I feel really guilty!" Priya sounds childish.

"What.... are you seriously kidding me! You want to go all the way to that café for such a small thing? We can get it some other day. Their staff is going to make fun of you, do you know that? You are honestly asking for a very stupid thing, P! If your parents were to hear you right now, they would start laughing at you! Imagine!"

Priya becomes sad and says, "I honestly thought you'd understand. You're literally sounding like you have no adventure left in you!"

"P, I have plenty of adventure left in me, just not for this small and silly thing! Frankly you're sounding like a 5-year-old right now!" Mira sighs heavily.

"Are you feeling, okay? You're a bit agitated right now? Is everything okay at your place? Did you have an argument with your family?" Now Priya sounds concerned.

Mira looks at her and says, "For the very first time, my father asked me a question, which he has never asked! I am as shocked as I have never been before. My mom is always aware of my whereabouts. I didn't understand what got into my father's head today!"

"What did he ask, Mira?" Priya's concerned tone is still there.

Mira breaks into tears....and says, "He asked where do I disappear to everyday without ASKING him!? I mean, is he not thinking straight? I am not breaking any laws; I am not harming anyone.... I am mostly with you, right?! And even today, I mentioned that I will be spending a night with you, he was like, then I should stay here forever!!"

Priya becomes excited and cuts her off, "M, that sounds like a fabulous life!! You and me, together! It's actually going to be great!"

Mira is touched with Priya's words; she thinks that she would too, love to stay with Priya. She wipes off her tears and says, "Forget it for now, we'll think about it tomorrow, our exams are over, and I have another reason to worry that our plan of going to Dubai is also cancelled. So, I am all yours! I will worry about it later, I mean I can't stay here forever, you know this and so do I...and..."

Priya interrupts, "Mira, I am sure your father must have had a reason for scolding you, he must have felt you're not there to spend time with him or something. He is a father who is concerned about his daughter, and because he was not able to talk calmly, also might be because he must be facing some issues in his office. This is just a tiny phase which will go away. So, don't be so hard on yourself. You can stay here with me for eternity, I won't say anything, but they are your parents. When fathers lose their tempers, mothers take a backseat! It's a life fact, remember. So, in case you're thinking that your mother didn't make him understand, it's only because he wouldn't have listened to her at that moment. Maybe, since you've come here, they might be discussing about the situation and how he talked to you. There's a possibility that he would call you, once he understands. So, give it time and now can we go and get that packed Maggi back, please?"

Mira feels better and says, "What's with you and that silly Maggi, Priya? Fine, let's go if you're so eager! Also, isn't it time for your car to arrive?"

"Oh yeah! I will ask my father, wait.... Or maybe after we come back from there then I will ask. Can we just go, or leave it?!"

As they reach the café, Priya finds the familiar bike parked right outside the café, her heart races, as they step in, there he is, holding the Maggi pack. He turns around and finds her standing there with pink cheeks and a wide smile. "Is this a coincident or what?! I never thought you'd come back to take this...how come...?" Sameer asks with a sweet surprising-husky tone.

Mira chimes in quickly, "Actually, she was after me to bring us here, to get the packet. Now I understand why she kept on insisting to come. She wanted to...." Priya holds her lips to shut her up and speaks, "I had no clue that you're going to be here. I just didn't want the maggi to go to waste, that's all."

"I completely understand, because it looks like this boy got it made some more and heated up the left over. I am touched with this gesture."

Priya still hasn't stopped smiling. Sameer hands her the bag and asks, "Do you wish to be dropped back again?" Priya gets tempted but firmly yet sweetly replies, "No, not now. I've come with her, and she is staying the night with me, so I wouldn't want to ditch her like this. Like you said earlier, next time. I will look forward. I have to rush home;

my parents are waiting. So, see you later." On the inside, she wants to go with him, but then she can't stop blushing. Mira is already in the car waiting for her. Sameer and Priya wave a goodbye at each other.

On their way back, Priya feels a bit sad, but then she gets butterflies by just thinking about the previous scene and smiles to herself. They quietly drive back, no stops in between. As they reach home, Priya thinks that she will empty out one of her cupboards for her friend so that, she can leave her clothes in the almirah and not have to carry them every time she comes to stay with her.

Priya gets to work. Mira asks her, "P, what are you doing and why are you emptying out your stuff from here?"

"I have just thought of something, M! And you know, once it comes into my mind, I just do it. So, I don't want to jinx it, stay quiet and help me, will you?" Priya is carefully placing her clothes on her bed and emptying the space. Mira realises Priya is emptying her cupboard to give space to her. She feels touched and holds Priya and gives her a tight bear hug, "You're the sweetest friend and my bestest friend I have never had. I adore you and wish we remain friends forever and ever, and not to jinx our friendship-in your words."

"You don't always have to explain yourself; you know. I understand you—always have, always will. We're together for a reason; it was meant to be. Now, let's wrap up this work and take a breather. It's been a hectic day for both of us. And hey, our exams are finally over! We've got a long break ahead—how about we plan something? A trip or a little getaway, just the two of us."

"Dude, you said what I was about to say! And BTW, a trip or a getaway are one and the same thing, hope you know that." Mira chuckles and adds, "Well before we plan that, I guess I will talk to my parents and you can take permission from yours."

Priya responds, "Sounds great, make use of our free time. And yes, I am aware that getaway and trip are TWO different words with different meanings, are you aware of that, Mira Rajput?"

"Well, my little miss English Conversationalist, please tell to me the meaning of the words-trip & getaway." Mira says happy-sarcastically.

"Well, thank you for the compliment, Missy. The exact meaning of the word 'trip'- usually refers to a journey which is planned in advance for leisure or work or even for education, which is why we use the term 'educational trip' and 'getaway' means an escape from your routine or monotonous life which is mostly for relaxation and even leisure. But also, trips could be longer and getaways are shorter. It's how you plan them. Get it?"

"Wow, you should become a teacher, Priya! You are seriously amazing! I mean you could pursue your education in a teaching course and do a Ph.D., and then maybe write a book, I am honestly serious." Mira sounds ecstatic.

"Just because I explained a simple meaning to you doesn't mean that I should become a teacher, babe. I want to go BIG! But maybe with time, I need to figure it out, find out the who's and how's of things. Then maybe we could both decide on something together. Right now, help me unpack your bag and set your clothes in here, will you?" Priya says playfully.

They both set up the cupboard, Mira feels really happy from the inside. Suddenly she goes, "OKAY, NOW TIME TO SET THE DATES OF RELAXATION...!!"

"SHHHHHHH...." Goes Priya. "What's with all the yelling?"

"I am super excited now, P! I am also pretty good in planning." Mira says excitedly.

"Calm down, honey, I understand you're excited and all, but first you are going to have to talk to your parents and take their permission, remember? I will certainly not even talk about the plan, till that matter is settled." Priya sounds like someone's strict MOM.

There's a knock on the door. "Priya! Can I come in?"

It's her father. "Yes, yes papa!"

"Bete, just a reminder that I've already arranged for the new car for you. I came by to let you know it'll be delivered in a few days. I need to get the registration plate and a few other things sorted before it arrives. I know I mentioned it would be here sooner, but your mom and I decided it was important to take care of these details first."

"That's okay, papa. All good. Mira is here with us so we are fine. I can wait." Priya replies chirpily.

Her father adds, "Once the car's here, you could always plan a quick road trip. Just make sure to plan ahead."

"Papa, we were just discussing that. But I was only telling her that she first needs to speak to her parents and take permission, then we will plan. So, I guess she will talk to them in the morning. Tonight, we are just going to relax and watch a movie or something, enjoy our holidays. It's been a long day." Priya says yawning.

"Ohh, you seem so sleepy, bete. Would like to share how your exam went today? Or maybe we can talk tomorrow. What about your dinner?" The new help is pretty good, thanks Mira bete. Please thank your mother from our end." Priya says, "No dinner, abhi, Papa."

Mira suddenly sits up. "Sure, uncle. No need to thank at all though, uncle. I will certainly convey your message." Mira speaks softly and smilingly, also seeming drowsy.

"Okay kiddos, enjoy yourselves." Saying this, he leaves.

"Want to watch HP series or some action movies? It's a bit too early for us to sleep. If we sleep now, we will wake up around 3 am. I seriously don't want that. The entire cycle becomes tumultuous. So, if you want to watch, then let's else, we should finish off the Maggi. That will be our dinner." Priya says matter of factly.

"Let's watch HP series. But I am not in the mood to have food now, maybe a bit later." Mira says dryly. "I don't feel like getting up now."

"Fine. I'll play the movie. I might finish the Maggi during the movie, then don't complain. And you dare sleep! I will push you off the bed if I see you sleeping. I mean it, missy!" Priya threatens Mira.

"I won't...! Look, I am not sleeping. I will watch. Can you just play the movie, please?" Mira is getting agitated.

"Hmmm. Okay, I will make a deal with you, I am playing the move, and if in case, during the first part, anyone of us dozes off, will have to wake up and shut the tv, and close the dvd player. Agreed?" Priya sounds challenging.

"Not fair, yaa, P!! You are sometimes so freakin' bossy, do you even know how frustrating that is?!"

"Well, yeah!! Because I love to irritate you." Priya sounds devilish. "Someone's cranky, how come?"

"I am not cranky, just sleepy and tired. I don't know what happens to me in your home, I just feel that I want to sleep in your place. I am not sure why. But I feel at peace when I'm in your home. It just feels nice and cozy and comfy, you know?!" Mira sounds snug.

"Alright babe. So, let's cancel the movie night for tonight, I would suggest, let's go eat something and then we can sleep. Might be that we won't wake up at 3 am, if we are full. Come on, let's go eat." Priya boosts Mira and pulls her up.

"That sounds like a good plan for tonight. Thanks for understanding. I will share the Maggi that you were boasting about so much. But I will not eat it cold, let's warm it up a little, please." Mira requests.

"I could warm it up for you, but I will eat as it is. I don't mind." Priya says coolly.

"Whatever suits you best. But let me tell you, outside maggi will never taste as good as home-made Maggi being cold. Don't tell me later that I didn't warn you." Mira says nonchalantly.

They both head to the kitchen, her parents are watching tv in the living room. Priya goes to her parents, and lets them know about their plan for the night. She tells her to call the guy-help to come and help. She refuses and Mira hears her say, "We would be finishing the left over maggi. I will warm it a little in the microwave. You relax." She comes back to the kitchen and finds that Mira has already poured it into two bowls, equally, and is about to put it in the micro. Priya comes and says, "Thanks, babe. Let me start it for you." And with a few clicks and rotations, she starts it. Mira asks, "Is there anything to drink with it, like a cola or a pepsi or something or even a juice?"

Priya opens the fridge and finds a 2-litre bottle of Thumbs up, almost half finished, she takes it out, "There you go, will this do?"

"Perfect." And while saying this, Mira shakes the bottle to check if it has enough frizz. Priya stops her, "Dude, it'll come out all on you! Don't do that!"

But Mira has already done it. As she was opening the bottle, it came onto her hands and a bit on her clothes.

"Ohhhh nooooooooo!" She goes, I am so sorry, P. I will just clean up this mess."

Priya laughs at her and says, "Dude, I am laughing at the thought that probably your sleep has taken a flight, and plus you aren't concerned your clothes are spoilt. Leave it, I will clean it up."

Mira says, "I just made a mess in front of you, I will clean it up dude! Seriously, you go check on the Maggi, please. I now know where the cleaning towels are kept.

Priya touches the bowls; they are pretty hot so she takes the mittens to shield her hands from the heat. Carefully she places them on the countertop, the rich aroma wafts through the kitchen. Mira is done with the cleaning as well. Priya calls out to her, Mira says, "I'll just be back, change my clothes and come."

Priya smiles and thinks, *'now she realises she wants to change'*. She sets the table with a plate and forks. Pours the remaining cold drink in the glasses, puts in a few ice-cubes and waits. After about 5 more minutes, Mira comes, Priya asks, "What took you so long, madam? You nearly took 10 minutes."

"I started to clean the stain.... like you said. That is what took me so long. Lets' eat. I am starving, now. Smells nice!"

They eat and enjoy their early dinner. Mira finishes first and still feels hungry, so she takes out a few slices of bread and butters them and toasts them in a pan on the stove, then she looks for some cheese slices or cubes, and some home-made chutney and tomato ketchup. Then on one slice, she smears a layer of chutney and on the other one, some ketchup, then tops it with a slice of cheese. And finally keeps the other toasted bread to make it into a sandwich. Priya gets tempted, and gets up to make one for herself. Instead of toasting, she keeps it raw, applies some butter, spreads some chutney on one and tomato ketchup on the other. Then she tops it with a cheese slice. "Et voila! Mine is better!" Priya states.

"Taste this.... you will fall in love with food with every bite!!" Mira challenges.

"Let's just enjoy and go and sleep. It seems you are absolutely wide awake, M!" Teases Priya.

"Well, if you say so...but if I hit the sack, I might just conk off. You never know. We'll see."

They finally finish their so-called dinner and wish the parents 'goodnight' and go to the room. Vedant is nowhere to be seen. Priya tries to check in on him, but notices his lights are off. She wonders why he has slept so early. She decides to catch him in the morning. Mira asks Priya, "Hey! Wanna watch the movie or should we just sleep, I think I can sleep right away. What about you?"

"Yeah, lets. I am way too exhausted to watch a movie now. So, I'll quickly brush and come." Saying this, Priya goes inside and starts thinking about the day and suddenly starts to think about her brother. She gets anxious and wants to know, as this has never happened before that her maggi was still left, or he didn't come out to hog her food. Something was definitely fishy or wrong. She didn't want to wait that long, so she quickly finishes off her brushing and comes out, goes out of her room, and sneaks in to her brother's room. What she finds was not really predicted by her then. She sees that he is inside his bed and playing on his PSP, a handheld playing device. She puts her hand on his head, literally scaring the shit out of him. "FUUUUCKKKKK, WHO THE HELL....!!!" He screams. Priya goes, "Control your tongue, bhai! I didn't know you'll be so bloody engrossed that you wouldn't know I am here."

"What are you doing here, didi? You seriously scared me." He responds, still shaking, probably.

"I just came to check if you were asleep, because you didn't come for dinner. Mira and me are ready to retire, I was just worried. And I didn't see you today. So...." Priya sounds caring.

"I am fine, and not hungry. Now go, I am busy. I will eat with ma and papa, if and when I am hungry. You sleep. Night!" He wants to get rid of her to get back to his game.

"Well, fine. Enjoy your game." As Priya is walking out, to trouble him some more, she turns on the light of his room and quickly rushes out, closes the door behind her. He probably doesn't notice, but she knows he will get back at her for this. She goes back to her room and hears some whispering. She notices a light under the blanket and then it suddenly turns off. She calls out, "Mira, are you okay? What are you doing? Were you on your phone, or talking to yourself? Although I've never seen you talking to yourself."

"Nothing, I wasn't talking to anyone, P. I was just looking for my phone." Mira lies.

"Mira, stop lying babe. What is wrong?" While asking her, she removes her blanket. "What is your reason to lie to me? I have never lied to you for anything...what is it you haven't shared with me? I won't judge you nor will I say anything, nor will I share with anyone. Just tell me, if there's a problem, I can help...."

Mira interrupts her mid-sentence, "Look, P. Can I just skip for now? I don't want to tell you anything. Everything's fine. Just turn off the lights, let's sleep. I will talk to my parents tomorrow and we'll make a plan for a getaway." She makes Priya's mood lighter. But Priya begins to feel suspicious and at the same time worried. She feels her headache begins to form.

Priya hesitated, her thoughts swirling in the quiet of the room. Mira's casual tone didn't match the unease stirring in her gut. There was something off, something hidden beneath the surface of her friend's words. The pain in her head sharpened, and she squeezed her eyes shut, trying to shake off the feeling.

"Tomorrow," Priya whispered, almost to herself. "Tomorrow I'll ask again. I need to know what's going on."

Mira rolled over with her back to Priya, her breathing evening out as she settled into sleep. But Priya lay awake, the weight of unanswered questions pressing down on her. Her headache pulsed in rhythm with the unease growing inside her. What was Mira hiding?

* * * * *

CHAPTER 10

A Trip with Mira

"Adventures are better shared with friends who feel like family"

The next morning, Priya tried to push the thoughts of last night's conversation from her mind. She told herself it was nothing—just her overactive imagination, a result of stress and too little sleep. But when Mira finally woke, her bright smile was almost too eager, too rehearsed.

"Good morning!" Mira greeted, stretching with exaggerated cheerfulness. "Ready to make plans for the getaway?"

Priya watched her closely, trying to read between the lines, but all she could see was her best friend, as normal as ever. No hidden glances, no nervous shifts in her posture. Priya's headache had faded, and the gnawing feeling in her gut seemed too quiet as well.

Maybe I was wrong, Priya thought, letting out a quiet breath of relief. Mira's carefree attitude felt genuine, and there was no trace of deception in her voice. It was clear that Mira just needed time to sort things out on her own.

Priya smiled, deciding to let it go—for now. "Yeah, let's do it. We'll figure it out together."

"First, talk and clear out the air with your parents, M! I mean it." Priya sounds firm.

"Whyy?! Can't I just let it be, P? If I talk to them, I might have to go and I don't want to have another break down, I don't have the strength for that." Mira becomes sad.

Priya pesters her, as last night's episode still hasn't really faded away from her mind. She realises she's been carrying the weight of it alone. So, in a way, things are even. In a way, they're both carrying something unspoken. Priya with her growing concern about everyone and everything, and Mira with whatever it is she's hiding. For now, they both stay quiet, pretending everything is fine, but the tension between them is palpable. Priya rethinks about their plan of a getaway, but then she perceives that she might open up during their getaway. She tells herself, *everything's fine. Nothing to worry. I want to go have fun with Mira. We'll enjoy. Stay cool, P.*

Mira comes rushing towards Priya, she feels vibrant and expresses her heart, "Oi, P! You won't believe how nicely he spoke with me, my father! He apologised for all he said, probably 'cause mom must have explained to him about me, how she's always aware of my whereabouts and I always let her know if I have any change of plans. I have sort of taken a flying permission from my mom, through a message, but I believe I will have to go home and bring some clothes for taking along and talk it out with them, face to face. It wouldn't look nice that I go without seeing them. Then my father would be travelling for work purpose and mom will get busy. So, my suggestion is that let's discuss where we are heading in your new car, and what all needs to be packed, and how long we'll be going for. Because, mi 'lady, according to you, a getaway is like a short trip, so whatever you wish to call it, discuss, decide and drive! Also, a thought, should we ask Saket as well? And how about Sameer? Huh?!" Mira says naughtily.

Seeing her so relaxed and happy, she pulls her to her room, and asks her, "Before we discuss and decide anything, can you please tell me what happened last night? I beg of you; please tell me why did you lie to me despite me seeing your phone light was turned on and you were whispering on your phone? I am anxious Mira! This anxiety is killing me, so please tell me, we are family and best friends!"

"Priya, you won't let this go, will you?"

"No way! You have to tell me. Can't you see I am worried and concerned! I mean, this kind of situation has never occurred before. You are ruining our relation by not telling me and lying to my face, do you even know that?!" Priya almost has tears in her eyes, and she is on the verge of bursting into them.

"Okay, okay, calm down babe. I will tell you the truth. So, I am being stalked by a guy. And he works at my father's office. I have been going to his office quite frequently as I like another guy there, so my father had his suspicion. And I wanted to get rid of the stalker-guy. I had to let my mom know, about the stalker, as he managed to get my number somehow and started to scare me by calling me, every day from a new number, and texting me weird messages. I showed them to my mom, she immediately talked to my father, and he lost it. At first, he thought it was me who was seducing him and stuff, then he found out from his office staff, and he was shocked to know that he had a psycho working under him. The other day when I came to you crying, that day he blamed me. I was shaken and broken. Last night, I came to know through the guy that I like, he called up last night to let me know that he has been chucked out. And right now, my father told me that he has kicked him out and taken everything of his including his phone, which actually belongs to the office. Last but not the least, he has been warned that if I receive any more calls or messages of any kind, he will be thrown in jail without any delay. This was just told to me. So, this is the whole story. So, let's have breakfast, then I'll leave and see you later."

"What was there to hide in this, can you please tell me? You were going through a distress and you didn't want to share with me, that is unfair. I would have understood, babe. No wonder you have been keeping so disturbed, lately. But I am right here. It is actually hurtful that you didn't want to share this kind of thing with me! Plus, you lied to me again, just now! But let me also tell you, I had an inkling that there was certainly something wrong. I had a very strong feeling. Yet....

Anyways, so, finally your problem is solved. And I believe the breakfast is ready." Priya shows a disgruntled expression.

Mira feels really guilty. She doesn't say anything then. They both quietly eat their breakfast, she gets up, goes to Priya's room to pick up her stuff, "I'll see you later." Priya then gets up from her chair, still eating, and sees her off. "We are literally behaving like a husband and wife. If someone weren't knowing us, they would definitely think so." Priya is trying hard to forget the recent event, but it has now come onto her face, still she tries to cheer herself and Mira, expecting her to at least apologise. But there is no such thing. Mira sits in her car and says, "I am extremely sorry, P! I really am! Please, please try and forgive me. I will come back and we can clear this unhealthy air between us. I promise to make it up to you. Just please don't be anxious anymore. Now, you go in and finish your brekkie, I'll see you when I come back." Priya nods her head softly, waves her goodbye and goes back in. She quickly finishes her breakfast, clears the table, and goes straight to her room to pour her thoughts in her diary.

Dear Diary,

It's been a while, I know. There's so much to tell you. Right now, I am a big pile of mushy ball, ready to roll in to bucket full of tears. First, I want to share the sad part of my news, then maybe if I pen down the happy news, I might cheer up. Lately, life has been weighing me down in ways I didn't expect. Mira and I have been fighting quite a lot these days. For some reason or the other, we have been arguing or have stopped talking to each other. I know last time it was because of me, but this time, she has crossed her limit.

It's still unbelievable for me.... D!! I felt really hurt. And on top of it, she hid the truth as well. She was going through a tough time, for some time, she didn't share, let's assume, she didn't want to share because maybe she thought that there was no solution or it couldn't have been resolved, but then why lie? She could have just come and told me- "Hey P, I am going through so and so problem, I didn't want to trouble you because there wouldn't have been anything we could have been able to do." I know at present while writing it sounds ridiculous, but then she could have just come and shared something instead of lying to my face! I am not being able to understand her thinking process. What she is expecting or what is going to happen to our friendship. Will it last like this...should I trust her enough? It's been hard to keep my spirits up. And some days, it feels like I'm carrying the weight of the world on my shoulders. But then, even in the midst of all this, there's a silver lining. I have met someone! I am not completely sure how far this thing will go...but at present thinking about him makes me hum... sing and dance even! He seems nice, humble, courteous, quite dashing, husky voiced.... I can never get tired of talking good about him. I am sure he must be having some flaws; I haven't seen them yet or maybe he isn't showing me at present. I will not want to jinx this relationship as of now, as it's just starting to build up. I just wish to see where it leads. But currently, it's giving me a great feeling. The weird part is, he knows I've had a crush on him, thanks to you-know-who else- Miss Mira Rajput! In many ways, I know she is an understanding person, and I am really glad that she and I are good friends, and I am also aware that all friends go through this kind of a time, but it hurts. And I shouldn't make it into such a big issue. So, I'll let it be.

Guess what, diary....my mood feels lighter now. So, thank you for listening to me...... I feel good!

Until next time.

Love, P

She keeps her diary aside, picks up her phone and begins to text Mira.... but then she stops. She thinks she would seem desperate or something so she texts Saket, instead- 'hi, wassup? V r plnng 2 go 4 a trip, smwhr.cr 2 join us in my new car?'

Within seconds comes the reply- 'congrats, bt can't...lvg 2 c my bro in 2 days. U gals njoy & miss me :-)

Priya smiles while reading the text. She again thinks to text Mira, but again she gives up and plans to go for her baths. She tidies up her room, places everything in its place and goes off to have her baths.

After a good 20 minutes, she comes out and sees Mira sitting there with her bags.

"What.... how...when...? Did you knock or something...? I was sorta texting you, but then I thought, I'll take my baths first. Thought you'd be busy with your parents. When did you arrive? It was so sudden; I thought you'll come by evening like you always do.!"

"I came 5 minutes ago, and I did knock before entering your room, I figured you must have gone for your baths, so I barged in, I apologise for that. And then you came out... Are you feeling better, now? Or should I apologise more and make it up to you? I can certainly explain but then can we please for once decide where we are going, if we are going?"

"Yes...yes...let's sit and search some nice places that we can visit in our car...somewhere close by...and I also texted Saket, he said he's leaving to visit his brother in a few days so he won't be able to make it..." Priya hesitates in speaking.

"Okay, no worries. We need a road map. But first let's decide where we are heading?" Mira sounds serious.

"First, tell me, how'd it go with your parents? Did they agree happily to you going solo with me?"

"Why else would I be here with my bags, bro?" Mira shrugs in an obvious way.

"Hmmm...great." Priya smiles. "So, I was thinking that we could either visit Jaipur, Agra, Rishikesh or some hill station, if we are wanting to get away from this heat. You decide and then we can search or take the road map."

"Priya!" Mira sounds sarcastic, "Why would you want to visit Rishikesh...there isn't much to do there, you just might end up becoming spiritual, is all!"

"Mira, there is no harm in that...is it? And as it is, we could get a chance to unwind by the Ganges, try some adventure activities like rafting or simply enjoy the peace and quiet away from the chaos of city life!" Priya says chirpily.

"I am not very keen, but if you say so. I suppose I'll give it a try. I'll go along with this plan. You could also think of Lansdowne; for the scenic beauty, the pine trees, the hill drive. Just give it a thought, will you. you have time till your car arrives. Please!" Mira pleads.

"Seems like you're actually not keen to visit Rishikesh... it's understandable. I honestly wanted to visit, but it's okay. If you really don't want to go there, I won't force. We both should be on the same page about visiting a place." Priya says in a low tone.

"P! I have an idea.... maybe we could visit Rishikesh first and from there we could head to Lansdowne...this way we get the best of both worlds." Mira says excitedly and pauses, then says, "There'll be a bit of adventure in Rishikesh and then some calm and beautiful views in Lansdowne."

Priya looks intrigued, "That sounds great, M! A road trip with a right balance of energy and serenity. Let's do it! I'll let my father know and he can help me plan."

Priya runs to her father and asks- "Papa, by when would the car be here? I believe we have decided where all we'll be going! Can you please find out or give me the number, I will call them and ask? I think we should leave by tomorrow or latest by day after, so in my opinion they should give it by tomorrow. And you also need to help us with the routes, so could you also give your road-map, please?"

Her father, momentarily taken aback by her words, breaks into a smile. Without hesitation, he calls for the car and while talking, he heads to his room to continue the conversation. Meanwhile, Priya returns to Mira to share the news before settling down at her computer to research the route and decide what to pack for the journey. This trip would be a completely new experience for her—traveling with a friend for the first time. She finds herself slipping into an excited, planning mode, carefully making a list of everything she'll need to ensure nothing is left behind. As she reads about travelling on the internet, she jots down the list of items that she thinks are immediately available at home like: Duffel bag(s), shoes, slippers, hers and Mira's driving license, first-aid kit. She goes to her washroom and checks in her medicine cabinet and makes sure that medicines like- antiseptic cream and liquid are there, band-aids, motion-sickness tablets, pain spray, cetirizine-anti allergic, paracetamol tablets, cotton and bandages should be packed. Then she goes to the garage and looks for some garbage bags to carry in the car and a pack of tissues. She finds a packet of paper plates along with spoons and glasses lying next to the tissue pack and takes them with her. She places all the things that she could collect on the floor next to Mira's cupboard. She goes to her computer and check the rest of the items that she thinks would be accessible in the house. She calls out her mom, "Ma!! Where are you?"

She yells back, "In my room."

Priya runs to her room and asks, "Ma, where are the umbrellas, the pepper sprays? I am not sure where they are, what I could find I've gathered. Also, I'll be needing the duffel bags, the brown ones that you bought last year."

"Beta, everything is in the garage-store-pantry. And why do you want to take the duffel bags, take a suitcase instead? It'll be easily accessible for you arranging everything in one place. Too many bags will be a hassle." She suggests.

"Mumma, packing in a suitcase will be a bit of a hassle as taking it out and carrying it around will be troublesome. I need duffel bags so that I can carry two separate sets of clothes. Everything has been thought of and planned. And miscellaneous items will stay in the car."

"Oh, I wasn't sure if you're going by car or by train... then all the more reason for you to take a suitcase...you don't have to carry it around and more space to keep your "miscellaneous" things!" her mother remarks.

"You are right at your end, ma...but please I want to take the duffel bags, I won't spoil them, if that's what you're concerned about. Please, ma!" Priya is begging.

"Alright, take them. I am aware you won't spoil them. But all I feel is it'll be too much for you to handle. Rest is up to you." Expresses her mother.

Priya happily goes to the garage to grab the duffel bags, Mira is talking on the phone to her boyfriend...she hears them talk and quietly goes around to scare her, "BOO!!" she goes and Mira screams, "EEEAAAAAAHH!!! Priya, you scared the shit out of me!" and quietly tells her bf who is still on the phone, "I'll call you later." And disconnects the call. “Why did you scare me like that, couldn’t you see I was talking? By the way, what are you doing here in the garage?”

“I came here to get the duffel bags. I am trying to plan for our trip together. Hence, I am collecting the things which are going to be required on the trip, unlike YOU, who is not at all concerned about ANYTHING!” Priya retorts and continues, “You should be helping me around instead of yapping away with your boyfriend!”

“Quit whining, P! You haven’t really asked me to help you. you’ve been running around the house collecting whatever, how am I supposed to help you when I don’t know much about your house?!” retaliates Mira.

“Dude, recently you said you know where most of the stuff is, while you were helping around in the kitchen the other day, now all of a sudden you have forgotten how things are done and what is where? You really need to watch when and what to talk! I am not the one whining, you are.... only because I didn’t let you talk to your boyfriend!!! How childish can you get, M?! I have had enough of your screaming at me, we are constantly arguing with each other! What is the matter with you? it’s like you are no more the way you were when I met you! we are literally eating each other’s heads every day of every minute! How long can this go on for? You really need to change your mindset. I have no clue what’s gotten into you. Just please tell me if you want to go for this trip or not, because I want to go, and I can convince my parents to go? And if you say yes, then you had better start behaving! So, you wanna or not? Be honest, please, M.” Priya sighs.

Mira sighs too, looks at Priya guiltily and says, "I am sorry. I want to go with you, and we will go. I am excited to go. You said you will let me know what your father is saying about your car..."

"Oooh, yesss, I thought I was forgetting something. Wait, lets' go ask together. Come!" Priya grabs Mira's hand and takes her inside. She asks her father, "Papa, what did the guy say about the car?"

"He said he will bring it home tomorrow morning. I had to really push him to bring it latest by tomorrow. I believe you are planning to leave soon after?" Her father asks smilingly.

"Not long now, Papa. We're leaving tomorrow! I can hardly wait! I've already gathered most of the things—just a few odds and ends left. Then it's packing, and we'll be on our way!" Priya says excitingly.

"Enjoy bachhe! Do you need any help in packing? Or planning? Let me know." Her father tells his daughter lovingly, as always.

"Not right now, papa. But I might need your help with a few things soon. For now, I'm just wrapping up some major and minor tasks," Priya calls out as she walks towards her room. She sits at her desk and notices her computer in sleep mode, the screensaver displayed. She presses the 'spacebar,' and the screen lights up again. Mira goes to Priya and looks at the long list that Priya has jotted down. She instantly reacts, "Dude, do we need this many things for a 4–5-day trip? Will we be requiring the umbrella or water? That would all be available at the hotels or even on the route that we'll be taking? How many bottles are we planning to take? Plus, the munchies, everything will be available at the Dhabas that we'll be stopping at. Whatever you need...and I hope you're not packing the food for the way because...."

Priya interrupts Mira, "Stop it, don't you say another word. We are taking our water bottles, not the crate, I am keeping some chips and biscuits, which I think will not be available, particularly these that we like, rest is a medical kit, because again, I know, you'll be the first to yell, "I got hurt here, I want a band-aid!"" Priya mimics Mira, again!

Priya opens the duffel bags to start putting in her clothes and blabbers to herself something. Mira looks at her doing her work, and asks, "What are you blabbering to yourself? Do you always do that?"

"I do it when I feel I have to finish up loads of things. Now stop disturbing and you too, get to work." Priya multi-tasks-talks.

While Priya does her bit, Mira goes to her car and takes out the other bags, and brings it to Priya's room. Priya looks stunned, "You already had two bags!?! Mira replies, "Well babe, I wasn't sure where we'd be going so I packed these extras. One has my winter wear with boots, one has summer wear with swimsuits and flip-flops and the other has casual and party wear with shiny shoes and heels. I brought them inside for you to help me decide what to keep and what to take."

Priya sits on the floor holding her head in dismay, "Mira, you can at least do this by yourself, honey? I have plenty to do.... toiletries aren't still packed. I have to pack my shoes. Right now, my mind is in chaos, I even have to iron my clothes. I honestly think that if you could just manage your bit by yourself, and let me do mine. But, if at some point you're not able to finish, I will certainly help you out. As of now, we only have till 9 pm, and it's already 5:30, I presume if the car comes at around 8 in the morning, we should leave here latest by 9, which means we should be ready by 8, to receive the car. Plus, the new car always has to go to the mandir, first. I would like to go with everyone, so I request that you kindly take care of your packing and help me out."

Mira gave a mock salute, grinning as she replied, "Yes, boss!"

She does as she's told, while Priya also gets busy in her task. By dinner, they are both almost done. Priya takes a big sigh of relief and so does Mira. She says, "I think all that is left to do is wait for the car to arrive and check everything."

"Hmmm...." Says Mira. "Priya, did you book any hotels, or should we do that when we reach?"

Priya gets up frantically, "Crap, I can't believe I forgot that.... how could I forget that!!!!??? Ohhh wait...weren't you supposed to do that, Mira? While you were hanging around, you could have made yourself useful by booking our hotels, dude!!! Now, our trip is delayed for infinity, I am sure! I wonder if we'd get the bookings! Shit!!! Shit!!! Shit!!!"

And there's a knock at on the door, "Kiddos, dinner is ready, how long for you both to join us?"

"Coming, papa. Just give us a few minutes, we'll be right out." Says Priya with a sulky look.

"What is wrong, sweetheart? Did you lose something?" he asks concernedly.

"No...no!" Priya shakes her head.

"Then, did you both not agree with something and planning to not go anymore?" Asks her father.

"Nnnnn...papa, you go, we're just coming." Priya says a bit annoyingly, but not rudely.

"Okay, I am going but just to let you know, I have booked you both a nice hotel in Rishikesh and Lansdowne, some has been paid and the rest I will give you cash, keep it safely. Now, come and finish your dinner." He surprises them. Priya gets up and jumps up in excitement. Mira is relieved.

Finally, they both tell each other that they are going, and there's no delay. They both go out and take their dinner and enjoy it, smiling and talking about their plans and how.

Next morning, Priya wakes up at 7 am. She has a smile on her face and tells herself, "*Finally we are going! We are going to find ourselves and understand each other, as I think I will talk to her and explain to her.*" She keeps her fingers crossed as she says this. She looks beside her; Mira is still sleeping. She wakes her up by calling her, "Mira, wake up, it's time. I am so excited. Get up, start getting ready. Then I will."

"Mmmmmmm.... gimme 5 more minutes, please. I'll wake up in 5, promise." Mira groans and turns to the other side. Priya warns her, "If I step into the bathroom, don't come banging, then. I'll take a good 20 minutes."

"Yeah, that'll be enough, I'll be awake by the time you come out, promise!" Mira sounds like she's almost up.

"Well, your choice and your loss. Suit yourself." Priya heads to the washroom to get ready. And before she steps in, she says teasingly, "Btw, my car is going to be here, everyone will be going to the temple! Hope you're coming!"

Mira opens her eyes just as Priya darts into the washroom, locking the door behind her. "Priya, you're such a cheater! This is so unfair!" Mira whines. But her words fall on deaf ears. Frustrated, Mira pretends to go back to sleep, though she keeps twisting and turning because, of course, now she really has to pee.

Giving up, she gets out of bed, heads to the powder room down the hall, and relieves herself. Feeling more awake, she returns to the room and lays out the clothes she planned to wear for the day. With everything organized, she decides to take a stroll around the house.

The helpers are already bustling about with their morning chores. Vedant's door is firmly shut, and she wonders if he's awake or still lazing in bed. Either way, she assumes he's either getting ready—or not. Priya's father is sitting nearby, fully dressed and engrossed in his phone. Priya's mother, on the other hand, is nowhere to be seen. The closed door to their room suggests she's still getting ready.

While she's still waiting for Priya to come out, she arranges her clothes in her bag nicely and organises the cupboard which has been lent to her, and keeps the unwanted things back inside. Then she cleans up the entire room by making the bed and plugs in both hers and Priya's phone to charge. Priya finally steps out and sees the entire room spic and span, she has her head tied in her towel, and the whole fragrance has spread in the room. "Wow, Mira! I am impressed! Thank you, honestly. You've done a brilliant job! I honestly thought you'd be asleep, and I will have to yell at you to wake you up! I am touched." Mira is all smiles and says, "You smell really nice, now my turn! It's 7:30 already, please don't leave without me!"

"Don't worry, I'll be sure to put in a good word for you with God!" Priya jokes.

Mira gives Priya a dirty look and steps inside quickly. "I will get you for that, missy!" she screams from inside. "Please don't leave without me!" Mira begs Priya.

"Goo, now don't waste time! I'll stall everyone." She chuckles.

Priya walks out of the room, still combing her hair and sees her father. She goes and sits next to him, "Jai jai Ram, papa! Goodmorning!"

"Goodmorning bete! Jai jai ram! All set?"

"Yes! It's confirmed na, papa? The car is on the way, already? Then what is the plan?" she asks excitedly.

"Yes baby. Once the car comes, we all go to the temple. And then we come back, have breakfast, you pack your sandwiches and we keep your bags in the car and then you'll be on your way. That is the plan." Her father replies normally.

"I am getting the goosebumps, now! Can't wait!" Priya starts walking back to her room and comes back to her father again, gives him a tight hug and says, "Thank you, papa. I love you; I hope you know that!"

"I love you more, sweetheart! I just want you to be happy. Bless you baby." He hugs her back.

She heads back to her room, searches for her diary, and decides to pack it. Even though she's unsure if she'll have the time to write, she tucks it into her knapsack anyway, just in case. Then heads to her computer and looks for a paper, where she had jotted down her itinerary. She doesn't find it, then she looks at the notebook where she was jotting the dos and don'ts of the trip, she still can't find the itinerary, so turns on her computer, and opens her word document. There!!! She finds it! She connects it to her printer and takes out a printed paper. She reads it to herself.

Day1: Reach Rishikesh hotel and relax. Be at leisure or go for some local sightseeing.

Day2: have breakfast, go for river rafting. Then go for trekking from there and set up camps. Or after trekking, have lunch in the nearest café. Come back to the hotel and relax. Have dinner.

Day3: have breakfast. Visit any of the temples. That will take up your time till noon. After that, you're free to relax, or go for bungee jump. Have lunch at the café or restaurant. Head to the hotel, or go for some shopping for local handicrafts or do some leisure activities.

Day4: Have breakfast and head to Lansdowne. Reach by late evening, have dinner and relax.

Day 5: have breakfast. Head to the lake side to enjoy a boat ride at the beautiful serene lake, surrounded by lush forests. Then one could head to a jungle safari. After the safari, head to the city's famous cafes and restaurants to have lunch and be at leisure.

Day6: have breakfast, attend the local festival which happens annually. Then head for some bird watching. Have lunch and head back. or visit some famous temple and leave for Delhi.

As soon as she's done, Mira steps out, smelling all floral, like Priya. She teases her, "Smell that, P! I also smell as fresh as you!"

"Great!" and ignores her tease and states, "So, I have prepared the itinerary for us, please take a look. I have outlined our trip in short. You'll have an idea. And keep it handy and safe, and if you lose it then I don't have anymore. But then I think I should get one more printed for me to keep safe and handy."

"Okay, I'll keep it safe. Right now, there are more important things to do. I will read it in the car, let's get ready and collect all the bags and take them out." Mira says firmly yet politely.

"You're right, M. then I won't take print out another itinerary, I will keep it in my bag." Priya complies.

"The car is here! Di! It's here!!" Vedu starts yelling all excitedly. "Come quick!"

"Coming baba!! One second!" Priya yells back to Vedant from inside her room. Then she tells Mira, "Come, let's go! We have to go to the mandir. We'll be late to leave for our trip then!"

"Alright, chalo! We'll finish up our last bit after we come back..." says Mira.

As Priya sees her car, she is overjoyed. The colour of her car is red from the door and hood, and black on the roof. It's all shiny and looks gorgeous. Since it's a Maruti vehicle, she loves it all the more. She looks at her father, runs towards him and gives him a tight bear hug, yet again! He too hugs her back, but then says firmly, "Let's go girls, or else I will not let you leave for your trip. It'll be way too late for you to reach, and I would want you to reach in the day time, not in the night. It's not safe for anyone to travel in the night. That's it."

As Priya's father says this, everyone gathers around the car to settle themselves in. Vedu inquires if he could drive his sister's car for once, everyone hubbubs together, "NO!"

Vedant raises his hands and has a guilt look, "No problemo!" he says.

Papa drives the car, and admires its pick up and gets accustomed to the car. Priya sits next to her father and everyone else sits at the back. Priya imagines getting accustomed to her car. She looks carefully at her father's driving-how he's changing the gears, and how he's sliding his hands on the steering wheel. Her father has a wide grin on his face as he's driving the car. She thinks and decides that she will let her father drive it whenever he wants to. In about 20 minutes, they reach the temple. The priest at the temple immediately understands what they are there for. He brings a silver plate along with some gangajal and some rice and roli. He tells one of them to bring some garlands and laddoos from the shop next to the temple. Vedant runs to the shop and quickly brings the items requested.

The priest performs his pooja and blesses the car and tells them to keep the flower in the car before leaving for a drive. Everyone obliges and fold their hands to thank the priest and Priya's father hands him some extra money, discreetly. This time Priya's driving the car back home and she realises the feeling her father felt when he drove. She loves the feeling a new car brings, how smooth it runs. As soon as they reach home, her father gestures the girls to get their bags and start putting them in the car. He actually doesn't want them getting late. Priya rushes to the room and first thing she does is keep her diary back in her drawer and in a hurry forgets to lock it. she thinks to herself that she might not get a chance to write in her diary. Then she quickly grabs all her bags and Mira grabs the rest. Priya's mother hands them a basket with some cold-drinks and sandwiches with some chips, napkins and a hand towel. Finally, they get settled in the car, her father wishes her a safe journey. He confirms if they both have their driving licenses and he also confirms that he has checked all the car papers, they are all there. They bid their goodbyes and Priya says, "Jai Shree Ram" and folds her hands and says that this journey should bring all good things.

Day 1: Reach Rishikesh before dark.

As they start their journey, Mira declares that they will take turns after every 150 kms. Priya states, she will think and contemplate about it and giggles. Mira gets bummed for a second and then grabs the cd album from the back seat and shows it to Priya. "Babe, these are for you. I have been collecting them since I came to know you're getting your new car. There aren't many but I believe these'll make do for our trip together." Priya feels really touched and she asks her to grab a brown bag which has some chocolates and a new fountain pen by Parker. "Where and how did you get this?" She asks excitedly.

"I have my ways, missy. I knew you have been looking to buy this pen since its launch. When I saw it, I bought it. hope you like it!" Priya says joyfully. She is simultaneously thinking in her head if she should speak to her about her behaviour or should she let it go for now. She knows in her heart that she is concerned about her but if she would understand is another case. So, for now she lets it go. Although she does have a weird feeling about the whole thing. She tells herself to stop thinking about it and keeps driving. Mira has played her favourite cd, ABBA. 'Take a chance on me' starts to play. The speakers have sub-woofers in the car stereo. She turns up the volume. Priya enjoys and gets more comfortable by arranging her seat and the wheel. She notices that the steering wheel has a lever which when pushed down, makes the entire wheel come down to a more precise level. "Ahha...this is perfect, now I suppose. I am so in love with this car, M! I am never getting rid of it.... never ever ever!!! This is my true love. I love you from my heart, my Jimny!" and she gives it a flying kiss. She even decides that she will decorate it her way. First thing she ponders is, she needs to buy the sun screen shades for her car. For the time being, she determines that she could buy them from the street hawkers at the traffic light stops. They will give a cheap thing for cheap, but then she will have to make do with them. They are about to exit Delhi, and still no sign of them. Mira asks her why she is driving so slowly. Priya lets her know what she is looking for. As they are about to take a turn to exit, Mira finds one street hawker holding the shades, they look to be slightly of a better quality. Priya tells Mira to haggle with the guy. Mira disagrees. Priya tells her to stay in the car and goes herself to bargain. She gets it for less, and she knew it. Mira teases her thinking he didn't agree for a less price, Priya retorts, "I got four pieces for a Rs.120. I wonder how much you must have bought them for!"

"Which means you got Rs. 40 apiece. Not bad, mam! I am impressed. Now let's see how long these last for!"

"You've challenged the wrong person; M and you are completely aware of that." Priya sounds bright.

"We'll see about that!" Mira chuckles evilly.

"Unless you have plans to ruin them, then I can't say anything. But this I can assure you that I will certainly keep them nicely." Priya replies confidently.

"Okay, now tell me this. Do we have plans to take a break?" Mira probes forgetting about the previous conversation.

"We've just started an hour or so ago, you're already asking to stop! How will we reach if keep stopping every hour, Mira. You remember that my father has told us firmly to reach before dark, else he will cancel out trip. He will call us back." Priya sounds desperate. "You know we have planned this trip for us."

"Yeah, P! I had just inquired that when we'd stop." Mira speaks politely.

Though Priya detects that Mira will lose it again, but she doesn't. To make the situation lighter, she tells Mira to grasp the food-basket. Mira lunges for it and brings it on her lap. "If you're hungry, you could have the sandwiches along with some juice or cold-drink. And maybe in another hour or so, we could stop for a chai at the Dhaba."

"Yeah okay!" Mira nods in agreement.

Priya continues to drive, Mira falls asleep. Priya takes a full advantage and drives faster; she crosses most of the Dhabas and doesn't disturb Mira. She drives well enough taking care of the bumps and rough patches. She reads the road signs and manages to take turns carefully, as she remembers the route her father explained to her. She stops a few times to check on the map her father provided her.

Priya drives till post lunch time; Mira has slept for a good 2 hours. As she wakes up, she tells Priya to stop for chai or lunch. Priya agrees and says, "Yeah, I think I need to stretch my legs and take a break."

"Now, you sleep. And I will drive. Let me also get the feel of this car. Let's find a good place to eat." Mira acknowledges.

Priya retorts, "I am aware what you're after, bro! I know your intentions, clearly! Anyways, I believe this seems like a good place to eat, a Punjabi dhaba. They must have lovely chai." She stops and parks her car. Beeps on the key to lock the car. The first thing they both do is wash their faces, and use the washrooms. Luckily for them, they chose a good enough place where the washrooms are at least clean, stinky yet clean. Once they are done, they order for some rice with dal and some curd with salad.

Mira asks, "How long till we reach? I am guessing another 3 hours or so?"

"Probably, depending on what your pace is. Just follow the route, don't take risks of taking a different route, because it's just straight down and then a few curves and turns when we are near our destination." Replies Priya.

Mira nods again, "Understood."

In mere 15 minutes, their food arrives, they relish each and every bite, but are unable to finish their food. Priya instantly requests to pack the left over and she decides she would give to some poor lady or man. They get up, pay and settle back in the car. Mira of course takes the driver's seat, turns on the engine, then turns on the music, fixes the rear-view, turns on the ac, and takes off. Priya decides to sleep, so she adjusts the seat in a way that she can lean and lie back. she becomes super comfy, and lets Mira drive. Mira lets her know, "I will need to know the route if I feel lost, P. So, please wake up for me when I ask you to."

Priya gives a thumbs up and falls asleep. Mira continues to drive well, also making sure that she is careful on the bumps and rough road. She comprehends that Priya is fast asleep, and she doesn't want to trouble her, so she parks the car on the side of the road and looks at the map to check where to turn, as she has come at a crossroads and is a bit confused. Priya wakes up as the car has halted. She asks Mira if everything is alright. Mira replies, "Everything's fine, just got a bit confused so confirming the correct route, is all. You go back to sleep."

"Telling me to go back to sleep will not help, M. Here, let me see. You keep driving...if it's not the right route, we will have to ask someone to guide us." Priya expresses calmly.

Mira does as she says. She continues to drive while Priya checks the map. She finds the path, and tells her to continue going straight. She adds that they are almost near their destination.

In about another 2 odd hours, they reach their destination. It's nearly 5 pm. They made it. Priya calls her father to let him know that they've reached. He seems surprised and happy at the same time. He says, "Well done, girls! Now go and enjoy. Just keep your phone charged at all times and stay alert."

"Sure, papa. Don't worry. I will keep you updated at all times." Priya assures her father.

The day was exhausting for both of them, so they just check into the hotel and organise their bags and lie down on the beds. Mira starts feeling hungry so she asks Priya if she is ready to eat. Priya says she craves for tea with pakoras and Maggi. Mira mouth starts to water. "Let's go then!" Mira sounds eager.

They head to the nearest restaurant and order for chai and pakoras. As soon as it comes, they hog it down so fast that they don't even realise that they were pretty famished. They ask for the check, pay the guy and come back to their room. Priya smiles at Mira and says, "Thanks babe for coming along. I am really glad that you're here with me! I would love for us to go places every year with you. Let's enjoy this trip."

Mira feels touched and hugs her friend. And blurts, "But what about when you have to go with Sameer? Will you still take me with you when you're with him?"

"I am not sure about that. But I am certainly sure that we will plan a trip with each other every year. That's a deal." Priya sounds promising.

Suddenly Priya's phone pings with a few messages. She checks her phone and there are about 4-5 messages from him. She checks and reads-

'Hope u're ok. I've bn worried sick. Couldn't gt thru. Whr r u? cn v talk?'

Priya lets Mira know about the messages. Mira tells her that she should talk to him once and let him know where you are if he's not aware. Priya's entire body becomes numb for a second. But then She calls him up and picks up in one go.

Priya- "Hi! What's up?" Priya tries to sound confident.

Sameer- "All good. I tried calling, but it was unreachable..."

Priya- "Where would I go? I am with Mira." She interrupts him.

Sameer- "I know. You guys are buddies. Where are you? Are you alright?"

Priya- "We are absolutely fine. We are in Rishikesh. I got my car today so we planned in such a way that we could get the feel of this new car. And plus, we needed a getaway vacation trip."

Sameer- "Sounds cool. You just finished your exams. That is great. Enjoy and be safe." He sounds caring. "When do you return?"

Priya- "Well, I guess Friday or Saturday."

Sameer- 'What will you do for this long in Rishikesh? Become spiritual or something?" And he starts chuckling.

Priya- "Not really, but after this we plan to go to Lansdowne."

Sameer- "Whoa!" He sounds impressed. "Which car have you got? May I know?"

Priya- "I got a Jimny. And I have fallen in love with this car."

Sameer- "That's brilliant. Alright, have a great trip. Buzz me when you return. Enjoy your trip. Take care and see you."

Priya- "Sure. You too take care."

And they hang up. Mira looks at her, "P, that was so cold. You sounded like you weren't into him anymore!"

"I like him, M. But at present there are more bigger priorities for me. And like I have said before, I am going to wait and watch. I cannot have the attitude that I want only him. Yes, I do get the butterflies just thinking about him and I would love to introduce him to my parents and everything, but for now I want to just enjoy and be independent." Priya declares. Then adds, "I want things sorted first. Like his future is sorted. He has his father's business, so his future is set. I have to decide and plan accordingly. If we belong with each other, I will be happy and if not, then at least I have my future to settle."

"I hear you, P. And I am glad and admire you. Probably, he respects you. So, I won't force you. Think before you decide, that's all I will say." Mira claims.

"Okay, let's keep it this way. So, for now, I'm exhausted, and I guess so are you. Let's sleep as we have fun activities to do tomorrow. I want to be fresh when I wake up, and you're coming too, no excuses." Priya declares.

Lights out, they hit the sack.

Day 2: Day for fun activities.

Priya wakes up at 7, feeling a bit fresh. She feels she wants to sleep some more. The room phone rings. It's a call from the reception- "Madam, the breakfast buffet is ready. You have an appointment for river rafting at 7:30. May I confirm?"

Priya is wide awake now. "Sure. We will be right down. Thank you." she tells the receptionist.

"Mira, wake up. They are waiting. Come on. Let's go have our breakfast, we don't need to take a shower now." Priya solicits.

Mira immediately opens her eyes. "I'm up. I woke up because of the ringing of the phone. You go brush..."

"No, this time we brush together. There's no time for us to work separately. Get up. we are late." Priya starts panicking.

"Calm down, P. I am up, look. Let's go." Mira consoles Priya.

They quickly change into comfortable clothes, brush and rush to the breakfast hall.

And they are to gather at the gate. Then they are explained that they will be taken in a minivan to the rafting point. Priya and Mira notice that there are a few newly married couples along with a couple of foreigners and some college boys. They whistle and hoot as they look at the girls. The man, Mr. Manoj, who is explaining about the rafting, sternly tells them to shut up. they still don't listen and the second time he warns them that if they don't stop their mischievousness, they will not be going. They become quiet for a while, and they start their nonsense yet again. This time Mr. Manoj picks up a stick and raises at them, tells them that they will not be joining this group. The boys don't feel sorry, but then they do as they're told. The group appreciates Mr. Manoj and applause for him. Then they sit in the minivan that takes them to the rafting point. Priya and Mira become a bit nervous, yet they have a sense of excitement growing in them.

As they reach their venue, they see that the speed of the water is such that for them as the beginners, it will be alright. But for the foreigners, it's a bit slow. Still, they all seem anxious to climb the boat as most of them will be separated and divided. So, Mr Manoj asks the girls and one of the newly married couples to be with him, then the other few married couples together and finally the foreigners in the third lot. Priya finds Mr. Manoj to be a gentle person. He seems like a content and a calm man who is aware of his job. They are told to wear the life jackets and the guards who had given them the jackets, tightens them. Finally, they too wear one along with Mr. Manoj and they head down to the valley to go into the boats. The boats are bright orange in colour, matching their jackets. Priya and Mira hold each other's hand and climb the boat. They don't let go. One of the guys pushes the boat in to the river and runs to climb it. The flow of the water takes them along. The girls scream at first, then they start to enjoy. They get a few splashes and then they are completely soaked. The water feels really nice. The married couples are also delighted. Priya wants to cherish the moment and memorise it for eternity. She realises that at this point she is the luckiest person. Mira looks at her and sees the thrill in her eyes and the smile that says is all.

"Do you know Priya?" Mira poses.

"What?" Priya replies.

"I have not seen someone so content, lively and fearless as you. Who are you, right now? I am honestly flabbergasted at this girl!" Mira sounds so flattering.

"How so?" Priya pretends to be innocent.

"Need I explain things to you? Don't act so innocent. I am getting to know you more and more every day. And let me tell you, girl, you are surprising me every single time of every day. And honestly Priya, I will always want to remain your best friend. And if ever, in future, Sameer tries to demoralise you or lets you down, I will know what to do. He should know you are one person he had better respect and love, because you're worth it. and I mean it." Mira becomes teary.

"Awwww, Mira. I was not aware that you have been trying to understand me all this while! And why do always bring up Sameer?" Priya sounds concerned.

"Because P, I am proud to be your friend, and also, I feel jealous of you. your nature, your fearless and bold attitude, 'Ye nahin to koi baat nahin attitude!' Your resilience, you never give up. I feel this way. I am not complaining nor whining, I too have a wonderful life. But it's natural to feel like I do. I don't know how or what you feel, but I am willing to tell people who don't know you, had better be aware that you have a friend like ME! Ha ha ha ha!!"

They both laugh it out. Priya thanks Mira for looking out for her and being there for her, with her. Mira adds, "And you're never thankless or sorry less. In simple words, P! You are a wonderful person!"

Their rafting lasts for a little more than 2 hours. Mr Manoj confirms if they would be joining the trekking later. The girls refuse, but the rest join the trekking group. They prefer to head to the hotel to chill and have a shower and relax. They have to take a cab back to the hotel as the bus that they came in was not just 2 passengers. Mr Manoj is kind enough to call for a cab and wait till it arrives. The girls thank him and they are on their way. It's nearly their lunch time. By the time they arrive, they are still slightly soaked. Like little children, they flip a coin to decide who goes in first. Mira flips, Priya picks, "Heads." And heads it is. Mira shouts, "We do best of three, whoever has more will go in first." Priya agrees. Mira flips again, "heads" says Priya. Heads it is again! Mira tells Priya to go in first. Priya obliges happily and teasingly. Mira sulks for a moment, then she climbs on her bed and plays with her phone. Her father calls.

'Hello, Mira! How are you bachhe? When are you returning? We miss you, beta.'

Mira sighs and replies, *'I am fine dad. We have this week to us. I will hopefully return by Saturday. I miss you all too.'*

'Take care. Be safe. Let me know if you need anything. Hope you're carrying all the necessary medications?' her father asks calmly.

'Yes dad. I have everything. And Priya is with me. So, you all don't worry.' Mira speaks softly.

'Just wanted to let you know, today we are going for dinner at Priya's. It's been a while since we've met.' Her father lets her know.

'That is nice, dad! Enjoy your evening. I'll see you soon.' Mira feels touched with her father trying to be there for her now.

Yes bete, you too have a good time. Also, I wanted to know, have you had a talk with Sameer? His father asked me when I came home today.' Her father inquires generally.

'No dad. Why what's the matter?' Mira asks in a concerned tone.

'I have a feeling he has found a girl for himself. Or he is out with his friends. His father hasn't seen him for a few days. He says, he just goes to work, does his meetings and goes to the factory, goes home, changes and then he is nowhere to be seen. You both used to hang out often, I thought you must be knowing about his whereabouts or his new interest.' Her father acknowledges.

'No dad! I haven't really talked to him nor have I seen him anywhere since last couple of days. If he calls, I will let him know that you all are looking for him. Is mom around? Can I talk to her for a minute, dad?' Mira's tone changes.

'Yes, here talk to her.' Her father hands over the phone to her mother.

'Hi mom! Why is dad concerned about Sameer's new interest? Why should anyone be concerned about it? I am not so why should anyone else?' Mira sounds diplomatic.

'Bete, his father has been asking around in the neighbourhood. He has been asking all kinds of questions like if they have ever seen a girl with him or has he been talking to someone...he has gone berserk and now our society has a new topic to gossip about. So, you have nothing to worry. You enjoy yourself.' Her mother sounds absolutely cool.

Meanwhile, Priya comes out of the shower. Mira is shaking her head in disagreement and utters that, "All women and their nonsense talks about others. When is this going to change, I actually wonder."

"What's wrong? What happened?" Priya seeks answers to her comments.

"Nothing. Can I just call Sameer?" Mira asks Priya.

"Why are you asking me? He is your friend first. That is pretty lame, M!" Priya retorts.

"Okay. I am calling him." Mira dials his number. "It's ringing, and I hope he picks up."

'Hello! Hey Mira!' Comes the husky voice. *'What's up?'*

'Don't what's up me. Do you happen to know what all is being talked about you in the society? Mira sounds annoyed. *'Your father is showing weird kinds of concern about you by asking in the society about your whereabouts and who you're seeing currently.'* Priya suddenly becomes attentive and comes and sits next to Mira trying to listen. Mira turns on the phone speaker.

He replies, *'No Mira. I am not at all aware, neither am I concerned. I am simply keeping to myself. I believe that shouldn't be anyone's concern. But yes, I will speak to dad. He's behaving like that probably because he hasn't seen me for some time. Don't you worry. Relax. I will take care of this. You gals enjoy. How's Priya?"*

Mira looks at her and Priya blushes and she gets up immediately. Mira sorta understands but then says, *She's fine. Didn't you talk to her last night?'* Mira asks excitingly, yet calmly.

'Yes, I did. But honestly, I feel strongly about her, Mira. She seems to give a vibe that even though she likes me but is playing hard to get. You know what I mean? And somehow, I like that about her.' Sameer sounds warm.

'Sam, I hear you. I cannot help you here. I will not come in between you two. My job was only to introduce you both to each other, and to answer your mindful question, I am not a matchmaker. How and where you want to take this relationship is up to you. Leave me out of this, please. So, we'll see you when we return. Mira raises her hand in surrender and is about

to disconnect the call…he suddenly blabbers, '*I am on my way, Mira. I want to see her. I will be there in a few hours. Just please don't tell her. Can you please keep this with you, just till I reach?*'

'*Yeah, okay. Bye.*' Mira disconnects the call. She lets Priya know that she is going for the shower and her mind is boggled with all that heavy talk.

Priya knows something's up. She wonders if she should ask Mira or not or should she call up Sameer and ask him. She becomes anxious. She doesn't know what to do. So, she just waits for Mira to come out of her shower.

* * * * *

CHAPTER 11

Priya's Acceptance of Sameer

"Happiness can exist only in acceptance."

Mira comes out of the shower. Priya is waiting patiently. She jumps out of the bed, and asks her, "What is wrong, M? Did Sameer say anything to you?"

Now Mira starts acting all innocent. "Nothing of this sort. Why do you think that? He just said that he will talk to his father."

"And when he asked about me, what did you say then?" Priya inquires.

"You were there.... didn't you hear?" Mira probes.

"Why would I ask, then?" Priya shrugs.

"Well, I just told him that you are in the shower and that's it." Mira proclaims.

"No, I don't believe you. I am 100% sure, he said something which made you become silent. Otherwise, you were all cheery and merry about today. I notice too, you see." Priya remarks.

Mira keeps mum again, and starts speculating what to say now. Suddenly she blurts, "He adores you, now. He has constantly been thinking of you. This is what he told me, to which I became speechless."

Now Priya speculates and can't find words. Mira exclaims, "I hope you get how I felt!"

Priya stares at her. All of a sudden, she gets a weird kind of feeling in the pit of her stomach. She doesn't understand whether she should laugh or cry. She gets a tingly feeling and feels good about it. But she can't understand what it is. She also realises that she hasn't had any headaches for a while, but now she has thought about it, she is likely to have it soon. She distracts her mind from thinking about Sameer. Mira interrupts her thoughts and speaks, "Hello! Should we go and have our lunch?"

"Yeah, let's go." Priya agrees in a way that she is a robot, and understands her master clearly.

Mira snaps her fingers. "Madam, where are you lost? Snap out, we are going for lunch. Sometimes I feel I have to behave like an elder one with you. I know, you feel the same with me, most of the times." Mira knows in her heart that Priya is thinking about Sameer. And she is going to get a big shocking surprise, and Mira herself will be left alone. Mira's phone pings, she knows who is texting her. She looks at the message, it reads- Hi! I'm almost here. I knw u're wid her, just share d name of ur hotel.

Mira texts back, 'v r in Anand Kashi. Shud I cm out?'

He replies, 'No need. C u in 5'.

Priya asks who Mira is texting. She replies, "Sameer just told me he has talked to his father and clarified everything. Isn't that cool?"

"Yeah! Nice! It's really sweet of him. I have the room keys. Let's go. I am famished. Aren't you?"

"Yeah, totally. Let's go eat." Mira sounds pretty casual.

They both step out and there's Sameer. Mira looks at him and then at Priya. She doesn't understand why Mira is staring at her, till she realises that Mira is signalling her with her eyes to look behind her. Priya turns around and cannot believe her eyes.

"What...the heck.... are you doing here? How did you..." Priya is gasping. I don't know what to say.... Hi!"

"Is that all you can come up with right now?" Sameer is proud to have given her a surprise. "A 'HI'?! I just wanted to see you." He gets off his bike, picks up the bouquet from his bike-bag, goes to Priya and gently kisses her lips. Priya is taken aback and so is Mira. She turns around and yells, "Guys, this is not the place. Could you both be a bit decent! Or get a room!!"

Priya is stunned and stands absolutely still. Sameer goes to Mira, hugs her and tells her, "Please cooperate, I am only here for tonight."

Mira is a bit relieved that the entire trip will not be spent alone.

Sameer then goes to Priya, holds her hand and asks her, "Can we talk? Let's go somewhere."

"Well, I would not want to leave Mira alone. We were going out for lunch. Lets' go talk there." Priya says.

He lets them know, "I will check in, change and join you for lunch. You gals go ahead or..."

"We'll wait here in the car. You go on." Mira tells him.

"What in the world was that? What just happened? I told you; something was fishy. I had a gut feeling that you were hiding something, Mira madam!" Priya taunts Mira.

"I simply told you, P that he adores you. Maybe you should have guessed it. He has specially come all the way to see you, because he wanted to. Give him the benefit of the doubt. He sounded desperate and he made me promise to not to tell you. What was I supposed to do?! Just hear him and decide. Probably, he doesn't want to wait any longer. He wants this relationship to work. And I can see he is already trying.

He likes your company and I think he respects you as well." Mira states the truth this time.

Priya doesn't reply now. She just smiles. But after a moment's pause, she expresses, "This feels ticklish in my tummy, M! I can't believe someone like him could fall for me. It's like all this is out of a movie. Should I continue to throw an attitude or should become soft now?"

"Keep your attitude, yet fall in love. Because he has fallen for the girl that you are now. You don't have to change for him or for anyone. Just be yourself. Remember what is right and what is wrong. Boys or men woo a girl by doing all these kinds of things and then expect to be treated like kings once they win the girl. But Sameer is not like that. He is different. I can assure you this much. He is a gentleman." Mira explains.

"Thanks, M. I have just realised that you know him pretty darn well. You both have been friends for quite some time. I am happy and proud of you sweetheart. I was actually misjudging you." Priya smiles and holds her hand. "And the way you have tackled our situation is really impressive. This shows that you don't break anyone's trust. I might be resilient but you are a responsible and a reliable person. You too never change for anyone. Because I love you for who you are, my best friend!" Priya says persuasively.

Just then Sameer comes back, he asks, "I apologise for making you wait for so long. Where are we heading for lunch, ladies?"

Priya takes the keys and says, "Hop in."

Mira looks at the map to check the location of the venue. She leads the way by telling Priya the way to the restaurant. Once they reach, Mira declares, "Just FYI, all the places here are purely vegetarian."

Priya enquires, "Are you telling or asking, M?"

"Actually, I am doing both. I am craving for a chicken curry right now, but I know I can't. We have to visit the temples tomorrow. So, when we are going to visit a holy temple, we shouldn't eat any animal. It's weird but true." Mira states.

They step into the restaurant. It's a huge hall that smells like a south Indian restaurant. A man dressed in a coat comes and asks them how many they are. Sameer, who comes forward to tell him, "Hum teen hain, sir."

The man tells them to follow him, and directs them to sit at a table which has 4 chairs. They settle down; Mira sits next to Priya and Sameer sits right across Priya.

Mira announces, "I guess now you guys should talk it out whatever you both feel for each other. Here, I have opened a window for you both to start your conversation in case you both are not able to. Now I won't hear or say another word. Pretend I cannot hear."

They all laugh at Mira's announcement, but they do agree that she did open the door for them to talk it out. Without any further delay, Priya says, "I'll go first. Let me thank you for your beautiful gesture of coming all the way just to see me. I am truly touched and have gotten to like you myself. But, please don't put yourself in harm's way. I love surprises, but not the ones which will hurt any of us."

"I assure you; what you're saying will not happen. Basically, when I cannot stop myself from thinking about someone or something, I just want to see it with my own eyes, even if it's overseas. I can also tell you this that I am a simple person, with no expectations. You and I will live our lives the way we are living now. All I want is you to be in my life forever, and just give this relationship a chance."

Priya gives it a deep thought. While she is considering, the manager comes with the menu card. They all go through the menus silently and Mira articulates that she will have rice and sambhar, whereas Sameer claims he will have idli and Priya also prefers sambhar and rice.

Sameer beckons the manager, and the manager tells a boy to take the order. Sameer lets the boy know everyone's order. Mira and Priya look at each other, Mira tells her to accept his proposal.

Sameer looks at Priya and then at Mira, "What's going on between you two?"

"Nothing." Says Mira.

Priya wants to say yes right away, but somehow, she is feeling a bit hesitant.

Sameer understands that Priya is a bit hesitant. So, he asks if he could hold her hand, she nods. "Well, there's the first sign of you accepting."

Priya's smile widens, a soft blush colouring her cheeks.

Mira also has a smirk on her face. Their food arrives. The guy is smart enough to distribute the bowls of sambhar and chutney equally. The bowls with rice are placed in front of the girls. They quietly eat their food.

Sameer pays, yet again. Priya can't stop thinking about all that he said. She is still contemplating. Mira observes her, but doesn't say anything. They return to the hotel. Mira tells Priya, "I would suggest you go with him and talk it out. I'll be in our room waiting of you to..." she pauses. "You get the idea." She completes her statement.

"Okay." Priya winks at Mira.

Sameer has already opened his room. He steps inside and Priya knocks at his door. He hears her knock and lets her in.

"I am not here for an entire night, so you will not take any advantages. I am only being clear. Plus, I do have feelings for you and I have accepted you. although I am worried about one thing, I don't want us to feel insecure in any way. I cannot take that."

Sameer pulls up the chair and makes her sit on the bed, while she's talking and listens to her. Then asks, "What kind of insecurity?"

"The insecurity that men get when their women talk to other men. I don't want to be questioned. It will not be an open relationship but a mutual understanding one. I am sure you are a great person, but these are my feelings. I might sound bizarre, but this is me. There I've said it all! Now your turn." Priya gets comfortable on the bed.

Sameer gets up, holds her face in her hands, and kisses her again. This time it lasts longer. "Thank you for accepting."

"That sounds too formal." Priya chuckles.

"I am genuinely truthful. And you let me know after two months, how I am doing as a boyfriend." Sameer smiles after he says this.

They both hug each other. She asks him, "You seriously came all the way to see me? You honestly had no work?"

"Yes. I came all the way to only meet you. You were way more important than any work." He replies softly.

"All in the mood for buttering, eh?" Priya teases him.

"Not at all." Sameer says innocently.

"Aww...I didn't know you were so innocent, Mr Sameer!" Priya continues to pull his leg.

They both laugh at this. And Priya tells him that she has to go back to the room, "Else Mira will not like being alone, any longer than this."

"How about you girls come here, we'll talk and then you both can go back to your room?" Sameer suggests.

"Let me ask her. We have the evening to ourselves. I'll let you know in a minute." Priya tells him softly.

She goes to her room and finds Mira watching television. She is constantly changing the channels, instead of sticking to one. "Hi!" goes Priya.

"Hellos!" replies Mira.

"So, Sameer is suggesting we go to his room." Priya tells Mira.

"Why?" Retorts Mira.

"He's just being courteous. You only mentioned that, remember?" Priya replies with a smirk.

"Alright. But tell him to come here, I have no interest in going to his room." Mira replied sullenly.

Priya calls him to let him know that he could come to their room. He obliges and locks his room goes to theirs.

"Hey Mira!" He says cheerfully. "How's it going?"

"All good." She turns off the tv. He settles into the chair, gesturing for Priya to sit on her bed. At first, the room is filled with quiet murmurs and polite small talk. Gradually, Mira takes the lead, sparking the conversation, and soon Priya joins in with enthusiasm. Sameer listens attentively before adding his thoughts, seamlessly weaving himself into the discussion. The hours slip by effortlessly, the atmosphere light and harmonious, free from arguments or raised voices. Lost in their lively chatter, they forget about dinner entirely and continue talking well into the night.

At around 4 am, they start feeling groggy, Sameer bids them a 'Goodnight', even though it's morning. He says, "Here, it's time for people to wake up, whereas, we are going to sleep. How and where the time went by is amazing! I had a good time, girls! Enjoy the rest of your trip! Keep in touch and let's meet when you get back."

"Will you leave without saying goodbye?" Priya jumps out of her bed and asks.

"Well, look at the time, I will not sleep now, have to reach the office, else you have just got to know about my father's tactics. For now, you go and sleep. I wouldn't want to wake you up. We'll talk, and you take care." Sameer holds her hand whilst talking to her.

"I prefer to see you off, it's rude otherwise. And I don't want to give the impression that I am not even a tad bit considerate. So, you go get ready. I will wait and see you off." Priya replies with affectionate certainty.

"Alright ma'am!" Sameer chuckles.

He heads back to his room but keeps glancing over his shoulder. She waves at him, urging him to go inside. He chuckles softly, flashing a warm smile before disappearing through the door.

Day 3: The day to visit the temples.

Suddenly, Priya lets out a squeal of joy, startling Mira from her half-asleep state. Mira bolts upright, groggy and confused. Priya turns to her with an excited grin and says, "Why are you dozing off now? It's time to wake up! Let's get ready. First, we'll see him off, then head to the temples to catch the sunrise. I've heard it's absolutely stunning here in the mornings! Come on, Mira!"

Mira groans, pulling a pillow over her head. "You're way too energetic for this hour," she mumbles, her voice muffled and heavy with sleep.

Priya yanks the pillow away, her grin unwavering. "Oh, come on! You'll regret missing this. Imagine the sunrise, the fresh air, and that magical glow over the temples!" Her eyes light up as she speaks, already brimming with excitement.

Mira sits up slowly, rubbing her eyes. "Fine, fine. But you owe me coffee after this," she mutters, throwing her legs over the side of the bed.

Priya giggles, pulling Mira to her feet. "Deal! Now hurry up. We can't miss saying goodbye, and I don't want to miss a single moment of that sunrise!"

As the two of them quickly take a shower and get dressed, the buzz of the early morning adds a quiet sense of anticipation. Priya practically bounces out the door while Mira drags her feet, still grumbling, though there's a faint smile playing on her lips.

Stepping outside, the cool morning air greets them, crisp and refreshing. The faint glow of the horizon hints at the approaching dawn. Priya looks around eagerly, her eyes sparkling with excitement.

They reach the meeting spot just in time to see him preparing to leave. Priya waves enthusiastically, her energy catching his attention. He turns and smiles, walking over to say a quick goodbye.

"You didn't have to come this early," he says with a laugh, glancing at Mira, who stifles a yawn.

Priya grins, ignoring his comment. "Of course, we did! Safe travels, and don't forget to call when you get there."

Mira mumbles something unintelligible, half-awake but offering a small wave.

As he leaves, Priya tugs Mira's arm, her voice brimming with excitement. "Alright, let's go! The temples are just a short walk from here. The view is going to be breathtaking!"

Reluctantly, Mira follows, the growing light of dawn casting a soft glow over the streets. Despite her sleepy protests, even she can't help but feel a spark of anticipation as the world around them begins to stir awake.

As they walk toward the temples, the faint hues of orange and pink begin to streak across the sky, painting a picture of serenity. Priya's excitement bubbles over as she quickens her pace, pulling Mira along.

"Look at that sky!" Priya exclaims, her voice filled with awe. "It's even better than I imagined."

Mira rubs her eyes and finally smiles. "Okay, I'll admit... this is pretty stunning," she says, her tone softening as she takes in the view.

The temple comes into sight, its silhouette majestic against the glowing horizon. The soft ringing of bells and the faint aroma of incense greet them as they approach. Priya clasps her hands together, taking in the peaceful atmosphere.

They find a spot on the temple steps to sit, watching as the sun begins its slow ascent. For a moment, neither of them speaks, lost in the beauty of the sunrise.

"This is worth waking up for," Mira finally whispers, her voice filled with quiet appreciation.

Priya beams. "Told you so!"

As the first rays of sunlight bathe the temple in a golden glow, they both feel a sense of calm and contentment, ready to embrace whatever the day brings.

As the sun rises higher, Priya stretches her arms above her head. "Alright, now that we've soaked in all this beauty, what's next?"

Mira glances at her, a teasing smirk forming. “Coffee. Definitely coffee. And maybe breakfast. You promised.”

Priya laughs. “Fine, fine. Let’s find a nice café. But after that, let’s explore a bit more. This place must have some hidden gems!”

They stroll back down the temple steps, chatting about everything and nothing, their spirits lifted by the serene start to the day. Along the way, they stumble upon a small roadside tea stall where a group of locals is gathered.

Priya insists on stopping. “Let’s try something authentic,” she says, her eyes lighting up.

Mira shrugs, still half-awake but willing to go along. The vendor serves them steaming cups of chai, the aroma rich and inviting. As they sip the tea, they strike up a conversation with an elderly man who tells them stories about the town’s history and legends.

Time passes without them noticing. By the time they leave, both Priya and Mira feel more connected to the place.

Mira sighs as they walk back toward their hotel. “You know, for someone who wanted to sleep in, I’m glad I didn’t miss this.”

Priya nudges her playfully. “See? I told you it’d be worth it. And this is just the beginning of the day!”

As they finish their chai and stroll back toward the hotel, Priya’s mind is already racing with ideas. She glances at a signboard advertising nearby activities and gasps.

"Mira! Look at this!" she says, pointing excitedly at a poster for bungee jumping.

Mira raises an eyebrow, her skeptical expression unmistakable. "No way. Absolutely not. That's not happening."

"Oh, come on!" Priya pleads, her eyes sparkling. "You said you wanted to do something memorable on this trip, right? What could be more thrilling than this?"

"Surviving," Mira replies flatly, crossing her arms.

Priya links her arm through Mira's and gives her a dramatic pout. "Please! You'll regret not trying it. Imagine the view, the adrenaline, the story you'll have to tell!"

Mira looks away, biting her lip, clearly torn. "I don't know... It's just so... high," she mutters, glancing nervously at the poster.

Priya grins, sensing her hesitation. "That's the whole point! Face your fears, Mira. Besides, I'll be right there with you. We can scream our lungs out together."

After a few more minutes of relentless persuasion, Mira finally throws her hands up. "Fine! But if I faint, you're the one carrying me back."

Priya cheers, practically bouncing on her toes. "You won't regret this, I promise!"

Soon, they find themselves at the bungee jumping site, where the towering platform looms over them. Mira's nerves kick in as they strap on their harnesses, but Priya's enthusiasm is contagious.

Standing at the edge, Mira hesitates, her heart pounding. “Priya, are we sure about this?” she whispers.

Priya grabs her hand and squeezes it. “Trust me. On three, we’ll jump together!”

Before Mira can protest further, the countdown begins. “Three… two… one!”

They leap, the wind rushing past them, their screams echoing in the air. The fear melts away, replaced by an exhilarating sense of freedom as they bounce back up, laughing uncontrollably.

When they’re finally back on solid ground, Mira collapses onto a bench, breathless but beaming. “Okay… that was insane. But I’m glad we did it.”

Priya grins triumphantly. “Told you! This is going to be the highlight of our trip!”

As they walk away, Mira shakes her head, laughing. “You’re trouble, Priya. But I think I like it.”

As Mira and Priya walk away from the bungee jumping site, still laughing and reliving the adrenaline rush, Priya’s phone suddenly rings. She glances at the screen and her smile falters when she sees her father’s name.

“Excuse me for a sec,” Priya says, stepping aside as she answers the call. Her father’s voice is sharp, and there’s an edge of concern that catches Priya off guard.

“Papa?” Priya says, a little confused. “I’m just out here with Mira, having some fun. Why—?”

Her father cuts her off, his tone more urgent now. "Priya, listen to me. I need you to cancel your trip to Lansdowne. It's important, and you need to come back as soon as possible. Something's come up. I don't want you to stay there any longer."

Priya's heart sinks, a sudden weight pressing on her chest. "What's wrong, Papa? Is everything okay?"

There's a long pause on the other end of the line, and Priya's eyes search the horizon, a sense of dread creeping over her.

"Just trust me, Priya. Please. I'll explain everything when you're back. But you need to come home right now."

Her father's voice is filled with an urgency that she's never heard before, and it sends a chill down Priya's spine.

"Okay, we'll pack our stuff and prepare to return by tonight," she says quietly, trying to steady her breath.

Hanging up the phone, Priya walks back to Mira, who's already watching her with concern.

"What happened? You look pale," Mira asks, tilting her head.

Priya shakes her head, forcing a smile, but it doesn't quite reach her eyes. "My dad just called. I have to cut the trip short. He said something came up, and I need to come back immediately."

Mira's brow furrows. "That sounds serious. Are you okay?"

"I... I don't know," Priya replies, her voice trembling slightly. "I just need to go back. He didn't say much, but I can tell it's important. I'll book my tickets right now."

Mira places a hand on her shoulder, trying to offer comfort. "Hey, it's okay. If we need to go, we'll make it happen. I'll help with everything. Don't worry."

Priya nods, trying to swallow the growing knot in her throat. As much as she wants to push the worry aside and enjoy the rest of the trip, she knows she has no choice. Something urgent has come up, and her father needs her.

The two of them head back to the hotel to pack up their bags, the excitement from earlier completely drained from the air. The weight of the unknown hangs heavy over Priya, leaving her with a mix of unease and a deep sense of responsibility.

The mood is different now—what was once a carefree trip has now turned into something more serious.

Priya takes one last glance around their hotel room, her thoughts heavy with her father's call. Mira notices her hesitation and steps over to her friend, offering a soft smile.

"You sure you're okay, Priya?" Mira asks, her voice gentle.

Priya nods, but it's clear she's not fully convinced. "Yeah, I just... I need to get back. Dad said it's important, and I don't want to waste any more time."

Mira places a reassuring hand on her shoulder. "We'll get to Delhi together, no problem. You've got this."

Once their bags are packed and secured in the back of the car, they head out to the parking lot. The drive back to Delhi is quiet at first, both girls lost in their thoughts. Priya focuses on the road ahead, but her mind drifts to her father's urgent call. What could possibly be so serious that he needed her back right away?

Mira, noticing the tension in Priya's posture, glances over at her friend as they drive through the winding roads of Rishikesh. "You're sure you don't want to talk about it?" she asks, her voice warm and understanding.

Priya shakes her head. "I don't know what's going on. He didn't tell me much, just that it was important. I hate not knowing."

"I get it," Mira says softly. "But you'll figure it out when you get there. You've always been strong, Priya. Whatever it is, we'll face it together."

They drive in comfortable silence, the hum of the engine filling the air. The landscape changes as they leave Rishikesh, heading toward the more bustling roads leading to Delhi. As the hours pass, Priya feels the weight of her thoughts begin to lift slightly, knowing she's not facing this alone. Mira is with her, and that gives her a sense of reassurance.

By the time they reach the outskirts of Delhi, it's late afternoon. The sun has begun to dip low in the sky, casting long shadows on the road ahead. Priya sighs as she glances at Mira, her nerves returning as the city draws closer.

"I'll be okay, right?" Priya asks, her voice barely above a whisper.

Mira looks at her with unwavering support. "Of course. You've got this, Priya. We'll handle whatever comes next. Together."

When they finally reach Delhi, the busy streets feel overwhelming after the calm of Rishikesh. Priya is still lost in her thoughts, her mind swirling with unanswered questions. Mira pulls into a parking spot near Priya's home, and the two of them sit in the car for a moment, the weight of the journey settling in.

"You want me to come with you?" Mira asks, glancing at Priya.

Priya shakes her head. "No, it's okay. I need to do this on my own. But thank you, Mira. For everything."

Mira nods, understanding. "I'll be just a call away. Don't hesitate, okay?"

Priya smiles weakly, her heart feeling a little lighter. "I won't."

With one last look at her friend, Priya steps out of the car and heads towards her home, unsure of what's waiting for her but knowing that Mira's support will always be there.

Mira unloads her bags and takes her keys and goes home.

* * * * *

CHAPTER 12

Secrets of Priya's Diary Unveiled

"Three things cannot stay hidden: the sun, the moon and the truth"

The day had passed in a blur for Priya. After the long drive back from Rishikesh with Mira, her mind was heavy with thoughts she couldn't share—thoughts about her father's unexpected call and the urgent need to return to Delhi. As she stepped into her room, the familiar surroundings felt foreign, almost as though everything had changed in the span of a few hours.

As she opens the door to her room, the first thing she notices is that it looks untouched. Nothing seems out of place. But then, her eyes flicker to the bedside drawer, the one where she had kept her diary. Her heart skips a beat as she sees that it's still open, just as she left it.

Priya sank onto her bed, her head still spinning. She glanced around her room, eyes landing on the small wooden drawer beside her bedside table. That drawer. The one she had kept locked for years. The one that held her deepest thoughts—the parts of herself she had never shared with anyone, not even Mira.

Different kinds of thoughts keep crossing her mind. She looks at her bedside drawer, again. Then she gets up and unlocks the drawer, but she finds it's open and not locked. Her heart skips a beat. She opens the drawer and finds her diary is missing. She looks all around, under her bed, in the cupboard, in her bathroom almirah, its' not there. Her mind starts racing, replaying the moment when she held her diary and she finds her hands trembling as she frantically checks her room again. She hopes that her diary would magically appear.

The reality of the situation hits her hard: her secret diary, the one thing that held her everything she had never shared with anyone, is gone! She feels a cold shiver run down her spine. The questions arise: *Did someone take it? why?*

He stomach churns as the truth dawns on her: Someone must have found it. The thought is chilling. She goes back to the time when her father called her to return immediately. *Could he have found her diary? Maybe that's why he called, because he read it.* The question hangs in the air like a thick fog. The possibility gnaws at her. She recalls the urgency in his voice, the way he had insisted she come back without delay. *Could he have read it?*

The thought sends a sharp pang through her chest. The diary-her secret refuge, the one place where she had written everything down, every hidden emotion, every word she couldn't say aloud- wasn't just an innocent collection of thoughts. There were things in there that only she knew, things she hadn't shared with anyone, not even Mira! If her father had found it, if he had read it...

the consequences could be far-reaching, more than she could ever anticipate.

Priya sits down on her bed, her hands shaking as she clutches the phone in her lap. Her mind races, replaying every conversation she'd had with her father in the past few days. Could he have been acting strange because he knew something? Was that why he was so insistent that she return to Delhi, why he had seemed so urgent, so out of character?

No, she tells herself. *He wouldn't do that. He couldn't have read it.* But the unsettling possibility hangs over her like a dark cloud, and she can't shake the feeling that her father knows more than he's letting on. Her heart sinks as she wonders: *What does he know?* And what's worse—what will happen if he decides to confront her about it?

Now, her mind isn't just worried about the diary being found—it's worried about what happens next. If her father knows her secrets, how will everything change? And more importantly, how can she possibly face him now?

A sudden knock on the door jolts Priya from her thoughts. She jumps, her heart racing, and for a split second, she considers not answering. But then the door creaks open, and there stands Mira, looking at her with concern.

"Priya? Are you okay?"

Priya forces a smile, though it feels tight and unnatural. "Yeah, I'm fine," she says, her voice unsteady. But Mira's eyes narrow slightly, and Priya knows she can see right through her.

Mira steps inside, closing the door gently behind her. “You sure? You’ve been acting strange ever since we got back. Is something going on?”

Priya opens her mouth, but the words don’t come out. The tension in the room is palpable, and for the first time in a long while, Priya feels like a stranger to herself. What should she say? What can she say?

She looks at Mira, feeling the weight of the truth pressing down on her. There’s no turning back now. *If someone has found the diary, the consequences are inevitable. She can only pray that she’s prepared for whatever comes next.*

Priya swallows hard, feeling the lump in her throat grow. Mira’s gaze is unrelenting, her concern now more apparent than ever. Priya wants to lie, to brush everything off as just a passing moment, but the fear gnawing at her makes it impossible. She hesitates, the air between them thick with unspoken words.

Mira doesn’t wait for her to respond. She walks over and sits beside Priya on the bed, gently placing a hand on her shoulder. “You know you can talk to me, right?” Mira says softly, her voice full of understanding. “Whatever it is, we’ll figure it out together.”

Priya’s eyes well up, her heart racing even faster. She’s not sure if she’s ready to confront this. She’s not sure if she even can. But the weight of Mira’s kindness, her unwavering support, makes Priya’s resolve crack. She takes a deep breath, the words barely escaping her lips.

"I think... I think someone found my diary."

Mira's eyes widen. She leans back slightly, her fingers curling into her lap. "Your diary? But... how? When?"

Priya lets out a shaky breath, rubbing her forehead in frustration. "I don't know. It was supposed to have been locked in my drawer, but when I checked, it was gone. I can't find it anywhere. And then... then my father called me to come back immediately. It's like he knew."

The room falls silent. Mira's expression shifts, a mix of confusion and concern crossing her face. She places both hands on Priya's, trying to offer comfort. "Do you think your father—?"

"I don't know," Priya interrupts, her voice trembling. "But I can't shake the feeling that he found it. That's why he called me back. And if he did, I don't know what's going to happen now."

Mira sits there for a moment, processing Priya's words. Then, she leans in closer, speaking with a quiet urgency. "Listen to me, Priya. We can't jump to conclusions just yet. Maybe he didn't find it. Maybe this has nothing to do with the diary. But we need to find out. If he has it, we have to deal with it, but we'll do it together."

Priya nods, grateful for Mira's calmness, but the fear still lingers in her chest, heavy and suffocating. "What if he knows everything? What if it's too late?"

Mira shakes her head. "Don't think like that. We'll figure it out. We'll talk to him, and we'll get through this."

Priya closes her eyes, trying to steady her breathing. Mira's words help, but the uncertainty of the situation still clouds her mind. The mystery of the missing diary, the sudden urgency in her father's voice—it all feels too much to handle.

"Let's get some answers," Mira says firmly, standing up. "We'll go back to your house. If your father is hiding something, we'll find out. But first, we need to make sure you're okay."

Priya looks up at Mira, nodding slowly. She feels a little less alone now, knowing that Mira's by her side. But the fear still lingers, and the path ahead feels uncertain. The truth, whatever it is, is waiting for her—and she's not sure she's ready to face it.

Priya takes a moment to collect herself, feeling the weight of Mira's words to sink in. She stands up, though her legs feel unsteady. Mira's hand on her shoulder is a grounding presence, but the anxiety still churns inside her. The truth, no matter how unsettling, is coming closer, and there's no escaping it.

She steps out of her room, finds the house is eerily quiet. Mira follows closely behind. Priya takes a deep breath and walks towards her parent's room. Mira grabs her shoulders tighter. "Priya, we need to talk to your father, you need to step inside!"

Priya nods but her mind is racing. The thought of confronting her father makes her go numb. *What if he's already made up his mind? What if him reading the diary has changed everything?*

She enters their room; her father is sitting on the chair and her mother is reading a book. He doesn't look up as she approaches. Mira stays out.

"Papa! Priya says, her voice trembling. He finally looks up, but his gaze is unreadable.

"Priya! Welcome back. When did you return? We never heard you come in." his tone is flat.

Priya swallows hard, her throat dry. She wants to ask him about the diary, to demand answers, but she's unsure how to even begin. Instead, Mira, who has been eves-dropping from outside their door, steps in.

"Hello uncle, hello aunty! We just wanted to talk to you about something important," Mira says, her voice steady, but firm. "It's about Priya's diary. She feels it's gone missing."

Her father's expression doesn't change. He doesn't flinch, doesn't seem surprised by the mention of the diary. Priya's heart pounds as she waits for his response.

"I know," he says simply.

Priya feels the blood drain from her face. "You... you know?"

Her father nods slowly. "I've seen it. I've read it."

The room goes still. Time seems to slow as Priya's mind races, trying to process the weight of his words. He's seen it. He's read it. The secrets, the confessions, the things Priya had kept buried for so long—he knows them all.

"Why did you take it?" Priya manages to ask, her voice barely above a whisper. "Why didn't you tell me?"

Her father's gaze hardens. "I didn't take it. But I know everything now. And it changes things."

The finality in his voice sends a shiver down Priya's spine. She's not sure what he means, but the fear that she's been dreading for so long is now a reality.

Mira steps back slightly, her hand on Priya's arm as she watches the exchange, but doesn't interrupt. Priya's eyes lock with her father's, the distance between them now greater than ever.

"What happens now?" Priya asks, her voice small.

Her father stands up, his expression unreadable. "We'll see. But things can't stay the same anymore."

And with those words, Priya knows that nothing will ever be the same again.

She asks again, with a slight shiver in her voice, "What part have you read, papa? Have you read it all?"

"Beta, I am shocked to know that you have been hiding this for so long, and you didn't think to tell any of us? You are our daughter, and you had the nerve to hide such a big and important thing!" His voice is now louder.

"Papa, there are things that the children do not want to share with anyone, hence they write their own thoughts in these things!" Priya says softly, with tears rolling down her cheeks now, pointing to her diary. "Can you at least tell me what is it you read, that you made me rush back?"

Her father's expression softens for a moment, but only for a brief second, before it hardens again. Priya's heart races, and she feels the weight of his gaze on her, as if he's searching for something within her—some truth, some justification. The silence stretches on, thick with unspoken words.

"Papa, please," Priya's voice quivers, her tears falling freely now. "I don't know what you read, but whatever it is... please, tell me. I need to understand. Was it that bad?" She takes a step closer, almost pleading, her voice barely above a whisper.

Her father's eyes narrow, and he crosses his arms over his chest. "It's not about what you wrote, Priya. It's about the things you've kept from me. The things you've kept hidden for so long." He pauses, his gaze drifting to the floor, and then back to her. "I read enough to know you've been carrying a burden. But you should've come to me with it instead of hiding it away."

The room feels cold, and Priya feels a tightening in her chest. This wasn't how she had imagined this moment unfolding. She had hoped for understanding, for some kind of explanation that would make everything make sense. But instead, she's left with the feeling of being judged—of having her thoughts laid bare, dissected, and criticized.

"I didn't want to burden you," Priya chokes out. "I thought it was my problem, my thoughts... I didn't want to drag you into it."

Her father sighs deeply, rubbing his temple as if the weight of her words is too much to bear. "You should have trusted me enough to share it with me, Priya. I'm your father. You don't have to carry everything alone."

There's a brief silence before Priya speaks again, her voice still shaky but filled with a determination she hadn't known she had before. "So, what happens now, Papa? Does everything change? Are you... are you disappointed in me?"

He shakes his head slowly, his eyes softening just slightly. "I'm not disappointed in you, Priya. But you've got to understand—some things can't stay hidden forever. You're not a child anymore. You have to start trusting the people who care about you." He steps closer to her, placing a hand on her shoulder. "I'll always be here for you, but you need to learn how to share your burdens with those who love you. Keeping secrets only makes it harder in the long run."

Priya looks at him, her heart heavy with a mix of emotions. She knows what he's saying makes sense, but the fear of her secrets being exposed, of being judged for them, still lingers in the air between them.

"Please, Papa... don't be angry with me," she says softly, her voice breaking. "I never meant to hurt anyone. I just... I was afraid."

Her father's eyes soften once again, and for the first time, Priya sees the glimmer of understanding in his gaze. He pulls her into an embrace, and for a moment, everything feels right again—like nothing else matters except this moment of reconciliation.

"I'm not angry, Priya," he murmurs, his voice low. "But you've got to promise me, from now on, you'll trust me. You won't keep things like this to yourself anymore."

Priya nods, the tears still falling, but this time, they feel like tears of relief. She wraps her arms around him tightly, knowing that while the road ahead might be difficult, she no longer has to face it alone. He whispers, "So, tomorrow, the first thing we do is, we take you to the doctor to get you checked."

She looks up at him and cannot stop crying now. Then her mother finally joins in and says, "This boy, Sameer, when are you bringing him home? He seems to be a nice boy, judging by your own words."

"Well, I would have shared this sooner, but I was not sure myself. He just happened to be a fling, which now turns out that it will be continued...." Priya smiles at her words. Mira adds in, "Well, if you meet his parents, you might not really understand them, but he is a very...... nice person. And trust me, there's more to him than you think!" She pauses, a playful glint in her eye.

"Well, then what are we waiting for, let's meet the boy!" Yells Priya's father. Priya shushes her father saying, "Papa, a while ago we were having a serious discussion, and now you have jumped on to this! I am not willing to get married, I hope you both are aware of this. Yes, you can meet him but nothing beyond that, please. I beg both of you." Priya is still trembling, but this time with some joy and excitement and a bit of nervousness.

* * * * *

CHAPTER 13

Sameer Meets Priya's Parents

"Happily ever after is not a destination, it's a journey"

"Nobody is getting you married right away. We are grateful, that you have found someone for yourself." Her mother replies, politely. "Just let him know that now we know and he can come and meet us, period."

"Ma, it's not that simple. It's not like you or he is in a hurry to settle down. We have just started seeing each other, we haven't exactly even dated!" Priya explains.

"So, we just want to meet the boy who you're going to date!" her mother confirms.

"Okay, you will need to give me some time, I will let you know when is the right time. He isn't prepared for this." Priya sounds nervous.

Priya and Mira head back to her room. Priya talks what is running in her mind, "How the heck did we manage this, Mira?! Look where it all started and what it has come to! My mind is playing games all over my head! What am I going to tell him, that we had a night together and now all of a sudden, my parents want to meet him! Does it sound weird or am I making it sound weird?"

"Calm down. We'll figure this out as well. I am amazed at the sight of your parents handling your 'life and death situation' so calmly! I mean, getting hold of a personal item is next to a life and death situation, exclusively! And by the way, what was that other thing apart from Sameer issue?" Mira asks apprehensively.

Priya turns to look at Mira, where she realises that she will have to let her know too. "Mira, the next issue that they came to know was that....I....I....I.......HAVE TO rush to the washroom!!" she runs to the loo laughing, before Mira can even grab hold of her.

Mira yells by coming closer to the door, "You had better tell me or loose me, missy!! I mean it. I know it is something serious. What goes around, comes around!"

"Wait, I am coming. Don't do anything, please. I swear I will tell you!" Priya yells from inside.

She gently opens the door, and softly speaks in her ear, "You don't have to threaten me like that, you know? I honestly don't like it."

"It's the only way you tell me the truth, baby!" Mira chuckles.

"Whine! Fine, the truth is that, I have been having these constant headaches. They are pretty severe, and they don't subside even by taking a painkiller. So that's what papa whispered in my ear, that first thing we do tomorrow is see a doctor. That's all." Priya says directly.

Mira becomes concerned and says, "Honestly honey, you are something else!"

"Why?" Priya asks innocently.

"What do you mean why? This is not something to be hidden." Mira repeats the words of her father.

"Yes, I get it. you really don't have to repeat. I understand that these kinds of things should not be untold." Priya says sheepishly.

"Alright." Mira pauses for a second and then asks, "By the way, did you find out who took your diary?"

"No yaa! How was I to know?" Priya sounds clueless. "But I could find out from Vedant. He must be aware." Priya's mind clicks.

She barges in to his room, the curtains are pulled in and he's busy on his play station, as usual. "Vedu!"

"Why did you enter without knocking?" he asks passively.

"Because you never hear me knock, that's why." She answers back quickly. "I have come to ask you something important, can you please turn it off for a minute?"

"What?" he pauses his game.

"Who took my diary?" she bluntly asks.

"The lady was cleaning your room, and the drawer that you left open, was probably completely open, the keys dropped, and while she was picking up the keys, she bumped against the table and something fell and broke. I think it was your favourite vase or a glass frame. So, mumma heard it and she went your room and found everything and also picked up your diary and took it. And then she called papa, and the rest is history. Now let me play, please." He speaks quickly so that he can get rid of her.

"Thanks, bro!" She walks out and closes the door behind her.

"Hmm...." She goes. And she enters her room, where Mira is eagerly waiting to hear the gossip. "So, who did it?" she asks excitedly.

"Well, now that I know it, it wasn't anyone's fault." Priya says nonchalantly.

"I want to know. Maybe I can help you in deciding better, who did it." Mira steps closer.

"No way, missy! Let's leave it at this. I can assure you it was nobody's fault. We move forward. Everything is clarified now." Priya tells firmly.

"Our next big assignment is convincing the boy to come and meet my parents. How and when will this happen?" Priya expresses her thoughts.

"One step at a time, P!" Mira suggests and calms her. "For now, let's just go to sleep. We'll think about it in the morning."

Later that night, as Priya lay in bed, staring at the ceiling, her mind refused to settle. The events of the day had unravelled in ways she hadn't anticipated, and the thought of having to introduce Sameer to her parents was both thrilling and nerve-wracking. She turned to Mira, who was scrolling on her phone in the bed next to hers.

"Mira, what if Sameer says no? I mean, what if he feels it's too soon, or worse, he thinks it's a bad idea altogether?" Priya voiced her thoughts out loud.

Mira put her phone down and turned to face Priya. "P, you're overthinking again. Sameer likes you—otherwise, this wouldn't even be a conversation. Just be honest with him. If he cares for you, he'll understand."

Priya sighed, hugging her pillow tightly. "I hope you're right. Because if this goes south, I don't know how I'll face my parents—or him."

Mira smiled reassuringly. "You'll be fine, Priya. Tomorrow's a new day. Sleep on it, and when you talk to him, just be yourself. Now, let's get some rest before your overthinking burns a hole in your brain!"

Priya chuckled softly. "Okay, okay. Goodnight, Mira."

The next morning, the sun streamed through the windows, and the chirping of birds signalled a fresh start. Priya woke up with a mix of determination and dread. After breakfast, she decided it was time to call Sameer. Mira gave her an encouraging thumbs-up as Priya stepped out to the garden for some privacy.

Her fingers hovered over the call button for a moment before she finally pressed it. The phone rang, and with each ring, her heartbeat grew louder.

"Hey, Priya! What's up?" Sameer's cheerful voice greeted her.

"Hey, Sameer," Priya began, her voice faltering slightly. "I... I need to talk to you about something important."

There was a pause on the other end, followed by his calm response. "Okay, sure. What's going on?"

Taking a deep breath, Priya explained everything—the diary incident, her parents finding out, and their insistence on meeting him. She tried to keep her tone steady, but her nervousness seeped through.

When she finished, there was silence on the other end. Priya held her breath, waiting for his reaction.

Finally, Sameer spoke, his tone measured. "Well, that's... unexpected. But honestly, Priya, I'm okay with meeting them. If this is important to you, then it's important to me too."

Relief flooded through Priya as a smile spread across her face. "You mean it? You're okay with this?"

"Of course," Sameer reassured her. "I like you, Priya. Meeting your parents doesn't scare me. We'll take it one step at a time, just like your friend Mira says, right?"

Priya laughed, feeling the weight lift off her shoulders. "Yeah, one step at a time."

After the call ended, Priya returned to the room, her face glowing with newfound confidence. Mira looked up expectantly. "So?"

"He said yes!" Priya exclaimed, her voice filled with joy and disbelief.

Mira jumped off the bed and hugged her tightly. "See? I told you it would all work out. Now, let's plan this meeting and make it perfect."

The days ahead promised to be full of challenges and surprises, but for the first time in a long while, Priya felt ready to face them head-on.

The following week flew by in a blur. Priya and Sameer decided on a day for the meeting, and as the date approached, Priya found herself growing more nervous. Mira, being her usual supportive self, stayed by her side, helping her pick out an outfit and mentally prepare for what felt like an interview rather than a casual meeting.

On the morning of the big day, Priya's parents were surprisingly calm. Her father was busy in the kitchen preparing his signature tea, while her mother arranged the living room, muttering about how the cushions were never in the right place.

"Mumma, it's just a meeting, not a royal inspection," Priya teased, trying to ease her own nerves.

Her mother shot her a playful glare. "It's the first boy you've ever brought home. Forgive me if I want to make a good impression too!"

As the clock struck noon, the doorbell rang. Priya's heart skipped a beat. Mira, who had insisted on being present as moral support, gave her an encouraging nudge.

"Go get the door, P. You've got this."

Priya hesitated for a moment before finally opening the door. There stood Sameer, looking effortlessly handsome in a crisp white shirt and dark jeans, holding a small bouquet of flowers.

"Hi," he said, smiling warmly.

"Hi," Priya replied, suddenly feeling shy. She stepped aside to let him in, her parents appearing in the hallway with welcoming smiles.

"Sameer, welcome," her father said, shaking his hand firmly. "Come in, make yourself comfortable."

Sameer handed the flowers to Priya's mother, who looked pleasantly surprised. "These are lovely. Thank you, Sameer."

The next hour passed in a surprisingly pleasant manner. Sameer was polite, confident, and honest as he answered their questions about his family, career, and hobbies. Priya's parents seemed impressed, and her father even cracked a few jokes to lighten the mood.

But just when Priya thought everything was going perfectly, her father leaned forward, his tone turning serious. "Sameer, I have to ask—what are your intentions with my daughter?"

Priya froze. This was the moment she'd been dreading. She glanced nervously at Sameer, who remained composed.

"Well, sir," Sameer began, meeting her father's gaze. "Priya means a lot to me. I won't pretend that we have everything figured out yet, but I can promise you that I respect her and care for her deeply. I want to take things at a pace we're both comfortable with and see where it leads."

Her father nodded slowly; his expression unreadable. Then, to Priya's surprise, he smiled. "That's a fair answer. I appreciate your honesty."

The tension in the room eased, and Priya let out a breath she didn't realize she'd been holding. Her mother chimed in with a light hearted comment, and the conversation shifted to more casual topics.

By the time Sameer left, Priya's parents seemed genuinely fond of him. As Priya walked him to the door, he turned to her and said, "That wasn't so bad, was it?"

Priya laughed. "Easy for you to say. You weren't the one being grilled by your own parents."

"You did great," he said, giving her hand a gentle squeeze. "I'll see you soon, okay?"

As she watched him drive away, Priya felt a strange mix of emotions—relief, happiness, and a tiny spark of hope. She turned to find Mira standing in the doorway, grinning like the Cheshire cat.

"Well, that went better than expected," Mira teased.

Priya rolled her eyes but couldn't help smiling. "Let's just hope it stays that way."

For the first time in weeks, Priya felt a sense of peace. The road ahead might still be uncertain, but she knew one thing for sure—she wasn't walking it alone.

That evening, as Priya sat in her room, she replayed the day's events in her mind. The meeting had gone much better than she had expected, and for the first time in a long time, she felt a sense of calm washing over her. Mira sat cross-legged on the bed, scrolling through her phone but occasionally stealing glances at Priya.

"You know," Mira began, breaking the silence, "for someone who overthinks everything, you handled today like a pro."

Priya smiled, leaning back against the headboard. "I don't know about that. I was terrified. But... Sameer, he made it easy."

Mira set her phone aside and turned to her friend. "That's how it's supposed to be, P. When you're with someone who cares about you, everything else feels manageable."

Priya nodded, her heart feeling lighter. She thought about how far she'd come—from the chaos of discovering her diary missing to this moment of quiet contentment. Her parents had accepted her decision to take things slow, and Sameer had shown her that he was willing to take this journey with her.

Later that night, Priya stepped out onto the balcony, the cool breeze brushing against her face. The city lights twinkled in the distance, and for the first time in weeks, she felt at peace. Her phone buzzed, and she saw a message from Sameer:

"Your parents are great. I'm lucky to have met them—and you. Sleep well, Priya. Goodnight."

A small smile played on her lips as she typed her reply:

"Goodnight, Sameer. And thank you—for everything."

As she put her phone away and looked up at the ceiling of her room, Priya realized that life would always come with its uncertainties. But for now, she was exactly where she needed to be—surrounded by love, laughter, and hope for what lay ahead.

And that was enough.

* * * * *

Author Bio

Pranjali, the author is loving and caring. A passionate storyteller, exploring the dynamics of relationships, emotions and somewhat self discovery. She draws inspiration from her life, infusing stories with humor and love. When not writing, Pranjali, spends her time in teaching English, and with her family. This book marks her debut into contemporary fiction, catching the joys and complexities of life and unexpected twists along the way.

www.ingramcontent.com/pod-product-compliance
Lightning Source LLC
LaVergne TN
LVHW041204150826
845673LV00001B/284

* 9 7 9 8 8 9 6 7 3 4 5 8 1 *